NEVER
Tell
Ben

Diane Namm

D0188558

BANTAM BOOKS
NEW YORK · TORONTO · LONDON · SYDNEY · AUCKLAND

RL 6, age 12 and up

NEVER TELL BEN

A Bantam Book / January 1997

Produced by Daniel Weiss Associates, Inc.
33 West 17th Street
New York, NY 10011.
Cover Photography by Michael Segal.

ISBN: 0-553-57045-5

Published simultaneously in the United States and Canada

Bantam Books are published by Bantam Books, a division of Bantam
Doubleday Dell Publishing Group, Inc. Its trademark, consisting of the
words "Bantam Books" and the portrayal of a rooster, is Registered in
U.S. Patent and Trademark Office and in other countries. Marca
Registrada. Bantam Books, 1540 Broadway, New York, New York 10036.

PRINTED IN THE UNITED STATES OF AMERICA

OPM   0 9 8 7 6 5 4 3 2

Prologue

MALORY HUNTER'S FINGERS shook uncontrollably as she dialed her mother's work number. The icy Nebraska wind whipped Malory's long blond hair around her face. She leaned into the phone booth, trembling with cold and fear.

"Come on, Mom," she pleaded through chattering teeth, "pick up!"

"Carole Russell," her mother finally answered.

"Hi, Mom, it's me, Chelsea."

"Chelsea . . ." Her mother immediately knew something was wrong. "Where are you?"

"We're having guests." Malory tried to steady her voice. "I'll bring the flowers. You get the bread. I'll meet you at the corner store."

Having sounded the alarm, she immediately

hung up. Her mother knew the code. She would call Malory's father, and soon they would all be "mobilized," as he put it. Shivering, Malory gathered her black down parka around her.

Frightened as she was, her thoughts went to her mother. She knew that at that moment, her mother was sick with fear. *Poor Mom,* she thought. *She just isn't cut out for this.*

Malory had to think fast. She couldn't afford to make a mistake—a deadly mistake.

She peered down Main Street. Traffic was slowing down from the morning rush. Most people were already on their way to work—heading toward one of the bigger towns nearby. All the high-school kids were already in school, and her twin brothers, Mike and Tom, had been dropped off at eight at their elementary school. Malory checked her watch. 8:35. The boys must already be in class, she reasoned. That made it more difficult. Now she would have to make up some excuse about a death in the family or something to get the boys out of school. Malory hated to lie, but it was the only way. . . .

She forced herself to leave the phone booth, teeth chattering and adrenaline coursing through her. The sidewalk was still icy from the last snowfall, and the ground was brittle under her heavy hiking boots. Fear threatened to scatter Malory's thoughts, so she concentrated very carefully on what she needed to do.

Avoid Lincoln . . . pick up the boys . . . avoid the house . . . back road to cemetery . . . act normal.

She slung her green EMS backpack on her shoulder and jumped onto her mountain bike, thankful that the roads were clear of snow and ice and well sanded. As she pedaled toward the boys' school, frustration welled up inside her—along with fear. The FBI had promised them they would be safe here! And it had only been a year!

Suddenly Malory had a terrifying thought.

Where *was* the FBI?

This time *she* had sounded the alarm. *She* had found out that they weren't safe anymore. The FBI had been nowhere in sight. It had all been up to a sixteen-year-old girl named Malory Hunter, currently known as Chelsea Russell.

And it was just luck. She shivered, pedaling harder. *Pure, dumb luck.*

Malory couldn't help retracing the morning's events in her mind. As usual she had left the house at about 7:45 A.M. to bike to school. At around eight she had stopped at the park bench across from the diner. She relaxed there, as she sometimes did before school, drinking a V8 and playing license plate poker with whatever cars stopped at the light.

Malory loved to choose license plates as poker hands. She had just gotten a JJR-88S—a pair of jacks and a pair of eights—on a blue Chevy

Blazer when she saw the black sedan. At first she didn't think twice about it, although a black sedan in Lincoln, Nebraska, was about as normal as a palm tree in Antarctica. Instead she focused on the license plate for her game. QQQ-33A. A full house. Grinning to herself, Malory looked more closely at the plate to verify her hand.

Nebraska license plates were white, with a comforting stripe of blue across the top. New York plates, she knew from experience, were white with a red stripe, utilitarian, and, in Malory's opinion, ugly. It was easy to imagine inmates making New York license plates.

This particular license plate was from New York.

In a flash Malory's eyes flew to the driver. One look, and she forgot all about her poker game.

The driver was ugly by almost any standards, with a large lopsided face that looked as if it had gotten its share of beatings. Even the man's head was battered looking, with hair growing in sparse patches on top of his bumpy head. In strange contrast to his repulsive appearance he wore a crisp, expensive, navy blue polo shirt. He stared straight ahead with a fake grin pasted on his face.

The man in the passenger seat was slender and small faced. He was drinking a can of Coke through a straw.

Someone else might have mistaken them for

4

undercover police officers. But Malory knew they weren't.

It was *them*. They were here. And it wasn't safe here anymore.

Malory trembled, thinking about the gangsters who had been stalking her family for as long as she could remember. Trying to shake the image from her mind, she pedaled as fast as she could to her brothers' elementary school. The great pines by the side of the road whizzed by, and she smelled pine sap and wood smoke. She reminded herself that Lincoln Hills was a calm and peaceful town, but as she neared Lincoln Hills High she felt herself getting more and more jittery. The men were probably already there, waiting for her to show up. Then what? Would they just shoot her dead in the parking lot? Or kidnap her? But thoughts like those didn't help. She knew what she had to do—and with any luck she'd have the time she needed.

Malory made a wide detour around the school, taking the back streets that had become so familiar to her in the past year. The men didn't know they had been spotted, Malory assured herself. She had just "faded away" from the park bench when she'd seen them, as her father had taught her to do. She was becoming a true master at the art of being invisible.

She checked the little rearview mirror on her bike. Nothing. She tried to relax. She would have to seem semitogether or Mrs. Carter, the elementary-school secretary, would never let her take the boys with her. If Malory seemed out of sorts, Mrs. Carter would insist on calling Malory's mother at work and getting an explanation.

Well, Malory thought, *let her try to call my mother at work.*

It had been ten minutes since she had called her mother from the pay phone and sounded the alarm. Malory knew that her mother and father would already be well on their way to the meeting place—the old cemetery just outside of town.

As she pulled up to the elementary school and leaned her bike against the brick wall, Malory took a few deep breaths. She reminded herself that she wanted to appear appropriately grief stricken over a family death, not panic-stricken about being chased by the Mafia.

"Mrs. Carter," she told the gray-haired woman in the school's office, "I'm so sorry, but I have to get Tommy and Mike. Our grandfather died this morning, and my family needs to leave to help make arrangements with the funeral."

As much as she hated to lie, Malory had gotten good at it over the years.

Mrs. Carter hustled off worriedly to track down the boys. As Malory followed her she peered out the hallway window into the street. There was still no sign of the black sedan. In the glass she caught a brief glimpse of her reflection—long, curly blond hair; blue eyes; straight nose; full lips. She wondered about her next incarnation. Would she have carrot red hair? Maybe a new eye color? Would she even be able to recognize herself?

When she reached the classroom, the twins protested at first. They didn't want to leave. Mike was involved in an intensely competitive game of Old Maid. "Just a sec!" he called to Malory, barely flashing his green eyes in her direction. Tommy, the prankster of the two, was playing a game of his own invention—"kiss the girls." The game was chaotic in nature, and if there were any rules, only Tommy knew them. As tense as she was, Malory had to smile as she watched him chase an assortment of screaming girls around the classroom, with his sandy blond hair standing on end. But this was no time for fun and games.

"Tommy." Malory grabbed his arm firmly and crouched next to him, whispering in his ear. "Tommy, I'm here to pick up the flowers." She didn't want to scare him with the code, but what else could she do?

Tommy froze. Then without a word he went over to Mike and whispered in his ear. The twins quickly joined Malory at the door.

"I'm terribly sorry," Mrs. Carter said. She obviously mistook the boys' frightened reaction for grief. "Will I see the boys tomorrow?"

"I really don't think so," Malory answered, quickly ushering them out the classroom door, out of the brick building, and into the biting cold air.

The boys grabbed their bikes from the bike rack near the door, and they were immediately on the road, pedaling furiously behind Malory as they all headed for the meeting spot.

Malory checked her watch. 8:55. The men in the sedan would have figured out long ago that she wasn't coming to school. By now they were probably on their way to the elementary school. Then they would go to the house or to her mom's work—depending on how much information they could trick out of Mrs. Carter.

Malory shivered. Her eyes went to the little rearview mirror again and again, but all she saw behind her were her two little brothers, pedaling as fast as they could.

Finally the old cemetery swam into view. Malory almost burst into tears of relief when she spotted her father standing next to their old white Chevy pickup. Her mother, she knew, was waiting inside.

Without a word of greeting, Malory's father swung all three bicycles into the bed of the truck, then boosted the boys and Malory up and helped them get as comfortable as possible on the hard metal. Before he pulled the big black tarp over them, he said to Malory, "We'll stop in four hours." And that was it.

Through a slit in the tarp Malory watched as they drove out of Lincoln Hills and left it forever. Lincoln Hills—the town that their FBI contact in the federal witness protection program had promised them was too small and so far in the middle of nowhere that they'd never be found. The town where they would, at last, be perfectly safe.

Safe, Malory thought bitterly. *Perfectly safe.*

But there had never been anywhere safe. From the time she was five and the boys were babies, there'd been no person, place, or thing that she could call her own and for keeps. The only thing she could rely on was her music—and they couldn't exactly lug around a piano. She realized with a pang that even the sheet music she'd collected was gone from her life. All of it was stacked neatly on a shelf in her room. *It's not my room anymore*, Malory reminded herself tearfully, choking back the sobs she could feel building inside her chest.

It was so unfair. No time to stop at home for any of her precious things. No time to say good-bye to her friends or teachers. Mrs. Solit, her soft-spoken music teacher, would wonder where she had gone. She'd worry for a few days, then just assume Malory was too rude to bother to say good-bye. And what about Melissa, the fifth-grader she tutored on weekends? Would she be able to find another tutor before her test next week? Malory sighed. She knew it wasn't her fault she had to leave suddenly, leaving no trace, as though she had never existed in the first place.

When is this going to end? Malory wondered miserably. *When?*

One

"HEY, WATCH WHERE you're going!" a boy shouted.

A rush of kids knocked into Malory, scattering her papers, notebooks, and pens as she tried to navigate her way through the swirling, noisy crowd of students on their way to homeroom.

Although it had only been four days since they left Lincoln Hills, Malory's parents and the FBI had already gotten her into the tenth grade at Roosevelt High in west L.A.

Lucky me, Malory thought grimly, watching her belongings ricochet off the lockers. It seemed to her that all 2,400 Roosevelt students were trampling on her things. And with expensive shoes. Malory scrambled to pick up her stuff without losing her fingers to the never-ending stream of pounding feet.

At least she was able to start on a Friday. One day of school was going to be traumatic enough. She would probably need the whole weekend to recover.

Carrying her books, notebooks, and papers in a precarious pile, Malory ducked off the main hall into a smaller corridor. There she leaned against the wall to catch her breath. A lock of her new black hair fell across her eyes.

The Black Crowes blared out of the classroom to her left. Malory looked up at the number on the door. 1034. Mr. Griffin's homeroom. Her first stop on another first day of school.

Malory couldn't stand feeling like the new kid, the outsider. But she had gotten used to it. In all the times they'd moved over the past eleven years, Malory had never once felt like she really, truly belonged—no matter how many years they stayed before they ran away again. Not in Lincoln Hills, not in Jacksonville, Florida, not in Saint Cloud, Minnesota . . . and she doubted it would be any different in L.A.

Malory peered into the open doorway and took in the scene. At the front of the room a tall man— Malory guessed he was Mr. Griffin—sat in the teacher's chair with his giant shoes crossed on the desk and his face buried in the *Los Angeles Times*. In the back of the room a crowd of boys and girls were piled onto desks, listening to a portable CD player at top volume. The boys all seemed to be

12

suburban kids dressed to look "street" with baggy jeans and baseball caps pointed backward. The girls looked like "Bubbleheads," in Malory's opinion. Bubbleheads wore miniskirts, platform sneakers, and cropped T-shirts—or anything else that was extremely trendy—and usually had their own credit cards and cars.

Of course, L.A.'s Bubbleheads were different from Lincoln's—mainly in how they dressed. It was early March—still winter back in Lincoln Hills. The girls back there would have on little winter schoolgirl outfits: gray jumpers and knee socks. But everyone in L.A. wore summer clothes all year long, Malory realized. The colors were fruity, bright plaids. Some girls were wearing spring colors: frosted pastels in cool grays and pale blues.

Malory took a quick glance at her own outfit. She couldn't help but feel out of place in her long-sleeved gray polo shirt, heavy black jeans, and thick hiking boots. Not that she'd ever dressed in a particularly trendy fashion or made a fuss about what she wore. In a way, she was so used to being an outcast that she hardly bothered to fight it. Suddenly she realized this was what she'd been wearing when they left Lincoln Hills. What with the three-day drive, stopping only to call the FBI, and helping her parents set up the new apartment, Malory hadn't had a chance to get any new clothes before starting school. At least it was clean, so she didn't feel like a total scrub—but her off-season outfit still made her feel like the Geek That Time Forgot.

The bell rang. All around her in the hall students scurried like cockroaches into their classrooms. In Malory's homeroom the noise level dropped considerably as headphones were plugged into the CD player, but the chattering and laughter continued at full speed. Mr. Griffin's feet stayed on top of the desk. *So that's it*, Malory deduced. *Homeroom is a study hall. What a waste of time. I have to show up, but there's no way I can get anything done.*

One thing was for sure—this place was nothing like her old school in Lincoln Hills.

"Are you looking for something?" Mr. Griffin flicked down the top of his paper and surveyed Malory over the top of his glasses. A wad of paper whizzed directly between them. He ignored it, without so much as fluttering an eyelash.

"Actually I think I'm looking for you. I'm—" Malory faltered. Despite her father's relentless drilling, she hadn't gotten used to her new name yet. "I'm Maddy Mailer," she finally got out. Mr. Griffin stared at her blankly.

"I'm new," she explained.

"I see. Pleased to meet you, Miss Mailer. Find a seat." The *Times* went back up, and from behind it he called, "Class . . . this is Miss Mailer. Please make her feel welcome."

The noise barely abated. The paper balls continued to whiz around the room. Only about ten kids looked her way. One boy in the back whistled. Malory ignored him and found a desk by the window near the front.

A few kids who didn't fit either the Bubblehead or suburban street category dotted the room. A girl with pigtails who seemed far too young for the tenth grade sat front and center, working intensely on something with a calculator. The boy who sat behind Malory was bent over his spiral notebook, working on an intricate doodle of some kind. All Malory could see of him was his wavy, chestnut-colored hair. He probably wouldn't bother her, she thought. Guys who drew in class were usually the quiet, computer-geek types.

The chatter had resumed full force, and Malory caught a few remarks aimed at her—just the way it usually happened. The girls in the back had taken a few minutes to assess her appearance. Now they were ready to let the world know what they thought of the newcomer.

"Charity case," said a piercing voice that belonged to a girl with a high blond ponytail.

"Get a look," remarked a brunette with black eye makeup and nail polish to match. A wave of their girlish giggles washed over Malory. *You've been through this before,* she told herself, fighting the feelings of anger and isolation that threatened to overwhelm her. *You can handle it.*

"Tough room," she muttered. She had a habit of turning her discomfort into a joke. It usually made her feel better. Most people didn't appreciate her sarcasm or wit.

She heard a soft chuckle from behind her. It was the doodler—but by the time she turned around, he had already gone back to his drawing. Had he heard what she said? Or was he just laughing at her outfit, along with the rest of them?

It didn't matter, she reminded herself. It wasn't as if she was going to make any friends in this class. Or in the school, for that matter. Her parents had always discouraged her from making friends. "It isn't safe," they'd say. Being safe was what mattered—even more than having friends and sharing secrets . . . not that Malory could ever share her secrets.

Malory took out her book for the next period—English. It was *Animal Farm* . . . again. No matter what grade or school Malory found herself in, it seemed they were always reading *Animal Farm*. Of course *Animal Farm* did have its merits. She always ended up becoming a temporary vegetarian when she was reading it. *At least it's good for my figure,* she thought, grinning to herself.

She opened up the book to where Old Major, the big white pig, sang "The Beasts of England" to the other animals. Malory, as always, tried to imagine the tune. The book said it was a cross between "Clementine" and *"La Cucaracha." Oh, my darling* cucaracha? Malory wondered. Before long she was humming to herself. It was a habit picked up over the many years of learning songs without a real piano, and she had never been able to break it.

"Catchy tune," a voice behind her said quietly in her ear.

"Huh?" Malory snapped out of her reverie. Then she realized she had been humming out loud. She could feel her face getting red. It was the first day of school—and now the guy behind her was on her case.

"I didn't realize they'd made a musical version of that yet," the doodler continued quietly.

Malory sighed. If there was anything she'd learned in all her times as the New Girl, it was that direct assaults must be dealt with immediately. But Malory had been hoping to put off her first major confrontation in west L.A. at least until lunch. Oh, well. She knew just what to say and do with these types. Put them in their place fast, and they'd leave her alone for the rest of the school year—or until it was time to move again, whichever came first.

Slowly and confidently, Malory turned to face her tormentor. . . .

And found herself face-to-face with one of the

most handsome guys she had ever seen. His brown eyes twinkled in amusement, and a lazy grin lit up his whole face. Malory's heart jumped. She hadn't gotten a good look at him when she'd first walked in. Suddenly she forgot what she was going to say. She felt the blood rushing to her face and quickly turned back to her book.

He's gorgeous, she thought with surprise. She turned a page of *Animal Farm* and pretended to read intently. *But just because a person has killer eyes, a cute smile, and fantastic hair doesn't give him the right to—*

"Excuse me," he said in a teasing voice. "Were you going to say something to me?"

Oh, great, Malory thought. *He won't rest until we have it out.* Indignantly she turned to face him, resolved to do battle.

He had not moved except to rest his chin on his hand. His eyes still sparkled, but now he was watching her with a quizzical frown. A curl of unkempt hair had fallen over his forehead. For some reason Malory had an almost irresistible urge to brush it from his forehead. *Get a grip,* she told herself angrily.

"Well?" he prompted. "Weren't you about to tell me about the musical version of *Animal Farm*?"

Malory suppressed a smile. "Look, you're obviously a very funny person—in your own way, I mean," she coolly insulted him.

He smiled. She found herself staring into his deep, dark eyes. This wasn't good. She was supposed to be putting him in his place. What was her problem? Flustered, she broke her gaze.

"I have a lot of work to do and—" she began. She struggled to find a crushing remark to end with but failed. "And that's that," she finished lamely, turning around in her seat.

"Well, I wouldn't want to interrupt your work," he said in that same low, teasing voice. "But you know—I *can* be pretty funny."

Malory hesitated. What was he doing? It wasn't exactly mean. Summoning her courage, she turned back to him.

"Prove it," she countered.

"What will you give me?" he teased her.

But before she could answer him, that shrill voice from the back split them apart.

"*Be-en!* What are you doing?" the girl with the high blond ponytail yelled over to him.

Malory took the opportunity to glance down at his sketch. She had expected to see crude stick figures or scribbling. But it was obviously the beginning of some kind of landscape. She blinked—but before she could make it out, he closed the notebook.

The ponytail girl broke from her group and skipped over. She wore a blue-checked miniskirt and a cropped white T-shirt. A necklace with pretty blue stones sparkled around her neck. Her lipstick was bright red. Malory suddenly felt as if she were much, much older—and plainer.

"Ben—we were waiting for you all night!" the girl squealed. "What happened to you?" She sat on the edge of an occupied desk and stretched her long legs out in front of her.

Ben, Malory repeated to herself. A strange, inexplicable thrill ran through her.

Ben looked puzzled. "What do you mean?" he asked, squinting at the girl.

"Last night, you idiot! Shella's parents were out! She had people over."

"Oh, yeah!" Ben slapped his head. "I totally forgot! I'm sorry, Erin." Malory watched him closely. He was definitely being sarcastic. Obviously he wasn't sorry at all that he had missed the party—but Erin didn't seem to notice.

"We had the most awesome time," she said. "Where were you? It was, like, so uncalled for!" She shook her head dramatically to indicate the depths of her despair. Mr. Griffin glanced up, rolled his eyes, and went back to his newspaper.

Ben shrugged. Malory thought he looked impatient—or maybe even annoyed. But Erin didn't seem to notice his lack of interest. She held her pose, which she probably practiced at home in front of a mirror to make sure it revealed as much of her legs as possible. Behind her the brunette with black eyeliner appeared.

"Really, Ben," the brunette scolded, picking

at her black nail polish. "Shella was totally bummed that you didn't show."

"Well, I'm, like, *totally* sorry, Emily," Ben said, "but I was doing my hair last night."

Malory could feel her lips curling in a lopsided smile.

"Yeah, right!" Erin rumpled his hair and laughed.

Malory turned back to her book. The girl was ridiculous. She didn't even know when she was being mocked.

Why would a guy like Ben waste his time with girls like that? she wondered. Suddenly she frowned. She had no idea what kind of a guy Ben was.

Before she knew it, the bell for the next class had sounded, temporarily deafening her and sending the rest of the students shuffling out the door. They all knew exactly where they had to go next. Malory, of course, had no idea.

Her heart sank as she saw Ben leave amid all the girls. Bending her head to hide her disappointment, she fumbled among the papers in her pack to find out where her next class was supposed to be.

English, room 2207. Malory looked over at Mr. Griffin, who was still completely absorbed in his paper. She wondered if he just read all day. Should she ask him where her next class was? Malory decided against it, figuring she might have to introduce herself all over again, and it just wasn't worth the hassle. Besides, she thought, she was a veteran at getting around a strange school. She should be able to find her next class all on her own, and hopefully before the whole period was over.

As she trudged up the staircase to the second floor, students raced by her on either side. She clung to her books and papers, assessing the day so far. She had made a classic entrance by dropping everything in the hallway before first period. She had met the usual cast of characters in her homeroom. It looked like she was going to read *Animal Farm* for the fifth time.

And there was this cute guy in first period who was kind of nice too.

Ben, she thought. *Ben what?*

It was silly to be thinking about that guy, but the more Malory tried not to think about Ben, the more attractive he became. Of course, he was way out of her league socially. As far as she could tell, he seemed to have his pick of all the girls.

But in any case, what did it matter? Malory shook her head. Friends were out of the question, let alone boyfriends. No attachments whatsoever. That was the bottom line. Attachments weren't safe.

Strangely enough, this thought cheered her up. If there was no point in trying to make friends in the first place, then rejection didn't seem half as bad. There was no way she could get hurt.

Malory paused outside room 2207. Her homeroom Bubbleheads had their lockers right across the hall from her English classroom. Erin, the blond ponytail girl, was carefully checking her lipstick in a mirror attached to the inside of the door to her locker. The brunette, Emily, was spraying her shaggy hair stiffer and higher. Another girl with sleek red hair chattered and laughed with them while she chain-chewed a whole pack of gum.

Suddenly Erin turned toward Malory and gave a slight jerk of her chin. Emily and the redhead glanced her way too, and then the three of them exploded into laughter. In spite of herself Malory felt humiliated. She bit her lip and turned toward the door to room 2207.

"Tough hallway, huh?" a familiar boy's voice asked.

She turned around—and there was Ben, leaning against the wall behind her. Across the hall Erin nudged the redhead, and the three exchanged whispers.

"Do you make a habit of sneaking up behind people?" Malory asked, her heart pounding. She busied herself with her schedule, trying to seem relaxed under his steady gaze.

"Not really," he said casually. "You just always seem to be in front of me. I mean, I always sit in that seat in homeroom."

Malory realized that this was probably true. Across the hall the girls whispered. Malory pretended not to notice, but Ben seemed to pick up on her mood.

"Those girls?" he said. "Once you get to know them—"

"Yes?" Malory said hopefully.

"They're much worse," Ben said, smiling.

Malory burst out laughing. The locker girls looked over.

"By the way, my name's Ben," he said.

Malory had to think. "Maddy," she remembered. "Uh . . . it's short for Madeline."

"That's a pretty name," he said simply.

Malory blushed fiercely.

"I have to go," she blurted, and ran into the classroom.

TWO

LUNCH PERIOD ON the first day in a new school was always the worst.

After standing on the hot food line for ten minutes, Malory got an up close and personal view of the grayish, gloppy macaroni and cheese and the greasy hot dogs. She decided instead on an apple and a bag of pretzels. From now on she'd bring her lunch. Looking around her, she saw that most of the kids brought their own or bought a deli lunch down the street at Deli-on.

English had seemed to last forever. The teacher had droned on and on about *Animal Farm*, often using the same phrases and words of Mrs. Lemana, Malory's English teacher back at Lincoln High. *They must all have the same study guide*, she decided.

During class her thoughts had kept wandering

back to Ben. He was obviously very popular—with the girls anyway. Well, who could ignore those eyes? Malory smiled. He was different—very different—from any boy she'd ever known. For one thing, he was smart and kind. And sensitive—he almost seemed to know what she was thinking. Yet he wasn't a geek. Or a jock. He was hard to categorize.

An artist, Malory decided. A creative spirit.

But then her smile faded. She'd made a total fool of herself in the hallway. She sighed. What did *he* think of *her?* Probably not much. She hadn't exactly made a great first impression.

She glanced around the cafeteria. The tables were all filled to overflowing with kids, talking, yelling, laughing, and goofing around. Everyone looked like they belonged, making Malory feel even more as if she definitely did not. Erin, Emily, and the redhead sat with some other similarly dressed girls and boys at one table that seemed to be the epicenter of the lunchroom. And the redhead was the focus of the table—obviously the leader of the pack. *That must be Shella,* Malory thought.

Instead of forcing her way into a crowded table filled with kids who didn't want to talk to her, Malory went through the lunchroom and outside into the school yard. To one side there was a lone bench surrounded by honeysuckle bushes.

26

Perfect, she thought, embracing her lonely lunchtime fate. *Well, there are two good things about L.A. No need for an overcoat, that's one, and two, you can eat lunch outside instead of dealing with the cafeteria scene.*

Munching slowly on her McIntosh apple, Malory's thoughts drifted back to her last home, Lincoln Hills.

Mrs. Solit would probably still be wondering where the heck she had disappeared to. Malory blinked, suddenly feeling a lump in her throat. The image of her music teacher's chubby little face with her sympathetic blue eyes and frizzy blond hair was an image she'd never see in real life again.

A voice from behind her scattered her thoughts. "I see you're on the macrobiotic diet too."

Malory looked around and saw Ben peering over the top of the honeysuckle bushes.

"Oh, hi." Malory averted her eyes, trying not to seem as excited to see him as she felt.

"Mind if I join you?" he asked—and without waiting for an answer, he pushed aside the bush and sat beside her.

"Still sneaking up behind people," she murmured into her apple, hoping to hide her blush.

"Then they can't run away," he countered. He polished his own apple on his chest. "So . . . do you have a last name, Maddy?" he asked.

Malory paused. The new name her parents

27

had told her to use didn't come naturally.

"Mailer," she said stiffly. It still felt awkward to say.

Ben stared deeply into Malory's bright blue eyes as he considered the name. For a panicked moment Malory thought he could see all the way inside her, past the dyed black hair and false name, right to the very heart of her—straight down to the Malory Hunter part, the part that never changed despite the numerous names she'd had to take. The probing look made her pulse quicken. It was as if at any minute he might say, "I know who you are, so why don't you stop pretending?"

But he just extended his hand and said solemnly, "Maddy Mailer. I'm Ben. Just Ben, as a matter of fact. Not Benjamin, not Ben Junior, not—"

"I get it, I get it." Malory laughed, taking his hand. "Just Ben."

When their hands touched, she glanced at his face. He seemed to have leaned closer. She pulled her hand away. Her heart was racing.

Ben cleared his throat.

"Move around a lot?" he asked. He bit into his apple.

"Yeah, well . . . um—I mean no," she stammered. "No."

He chuckled. "Well, which is it?"

"Some, not much," Malory murmured

distractedly. She opened her purse and began fumbling through it for no reason at all. "What about you?"

"Me?" Ben leaned back on the bench, eating his apple, and eyed the school philosophically. "Nope, I was born here, raised here, and if I'm extremely unlucky, I may live here my entire life."

"You like traveling?"

"Theoretically." He smiled at her. Once again Malory's heart fluttered. Her hands kept rooting desperately through her belongings. He really had incredible eyes. And hair you wanted to run your hands through, and . . .

"So, where are you from?" he asked.

"Oh, lots of places." Malory gave him the standard answer, then changed the subject. "So you draw, I guess?"

"Yeah," he answered. "And just what are you looking for in that bag?"

Malory looked up. His eyes twinkled. Her face felt hot. She took out the first thing her fingers felt.

"This!" It was lip gloss.

"I see. A furious search for lipstick."

"It's gloss, for chapped lips. I have very chapped lips. Well, they're going to be chapped. If I don't use my gloss." *Oh, my God, Mal,* she thought, *stop babbling!*

"I see. Well, you wouldn't want that." He grinned.

Malory clumsily rubbed some gloss on her lips, then shoved the stick back in her bag.

"Must be kind of hard to make friends when you move around so much," he said casually. Malory felt the blush rise up again to her cheeks. She couldn't control it. If only he weren't so sympathetic and kind.

"Well . . ." She trailed off vaguely and squinted across the school yard, as if something very interesting was over there.

"It's tough even when you don't move around," he said in a faraway voice.

Malory stole a quick glance at him. "What do you mean?" she found herself asking.

Ben cocked his head and looked closely at her. "Well . . . L.A. is a strange place. Everyone here spends a lot of time by themselves, with only a phone and a car linking them to the outside world. So when you finally *do* get out, you want to make a good impression on the other shut-ins. You get a nice car and nice clothes and nice hair and . . . well, I guess it gets to be a way of life. You know what I mean?"

Malory laughed. "Yeah," she said. She felt so easy and comfortable talking to him; it was the first time she'd felt at peace all week. "So—"

But before she could say any more, a tall blond guy walked over to where they were sitting. He was wearing shorts, a T-shirt, and Tevas. With his tousled hair, he looked like the classic surfer. Malory thought she had seen him sitting at the Bubbleheads' lunch table.

"Yo, Ben—what are you doing out here? You ditched us for lunch."

Ben glanced quickly at Malory and then looked back to his friend. Malory thought she saw his face redden. *No, that's probably just wishful thinking,* she told herself.

"Oh, sorry, man—I just forgot. It was so nice out here and—" Ben looked back to Malory and smiled as he paused. She felt chills go down her spine. "Seth, this is Maddy. Maddy, Seth."

"Hi," Malory said pleasantly.

"Nice to meet you." Seth smiled at Malory. He looked back to Ben. "It's no big deal. We just wondered where you were—then I thought I saw you sitting out here, so I came to hassle you."

Ben and Malory both laughed. "I appreciate that," Ben said.

"Yeah, I'm sure you do." Seth sat down next to Ben. "But no worries; a girl is always an acceptable excuse for missing lunch with the guys." Now Malory was the one to blush. Seth was only kidding, but she couldn't help wondering if there really were lots of other girls that Ben spent his time with. "You new here?" Seth asked her.

"Yes." Malory hoped he didn't ask her a lot of questions.

"Where did you come from?"

Just when she thought she would have to go

on with her lies once again, she was saved by the bell. Lunch was over. She gathered her things for class. "I gotta go to math. I don't want to be late on the first day. See you later," she said to them. They both said "Bye" as she walked away. She looked over her shoulder and snuck one last look at Ben—he was smiling at her. She smiled back. Maybe she hadn't made a complete fool of herself after all.

Malory made it through the rest of her afternoon classes, impatient for the last period of the day—music appreciation. Here at last she'd be able to lose herself in the thing she loved the most, the thing that never let her down—music.

In spite of her better judgment, she was hoping there might be an old school piano she could play . . . maybe even for the school orchestra. By the time music appreciation rolled around, she could barely contain her excitement at the prospect of actually sitting down at a keyboard.

Most of the class was spent going over a test the class had taken the day before. Then Mrs. Lerner rapped her music stand with a conductor's baton for attention, her curly brown hair bouncing with every tap.

"I want you all to listen very carefully to this excerpt of Beethoven's Ninth Symphony," she said, smiling encouragingly as she pointed her baton. Malory already liked Mrs. Lerner. By the way the other kids acted, Malory could tell she was a popular teacher.

Then Mrs. Lerner turned on the tape machine, and all at once Malory was lost in the crashing sounds of the beautiful symphony. The hassles of being the new girl, her fears about those men that were after her family—all Malory's worries floated out of her head. Her body seemed to absorb the music as it ebbed and flowed around her.

Then suddenly the music stopped.

Mrs. Lerner looked quizzically at the class.

"Can someone take a guess as to how Beethoven was able to compose this symphony, despite the fact that he was deaf?" she asked.

A heavy silence filled the classroom, and a few goofy-looking guys in the corner snorted in embarrassment. No one raised a hand.

Mrs. Lerner consulted her class list.

"Mister . . . Raymond. Care to hazard a guess?" A tall Asian kid in the back jumped at being called on.

"Um . . . well, maybe he didn't care how it sounded . . . ?" The kid looked hopeful.

Mrs. Lerner smiled. "An interesting theory, Mr. Raymond, but no."

A hand went up across the room.

"Yes, Miss Ippolito," Mrs. Lerner said. "Enlighten us."

"Well, for starters," began the girl, who had short blond hair. "Mr. Beethoven was extremely jealous of Italian composers of the time—"

"Yes, I believe we've heard this argument before from you, thank you." Mrs. Lerner rolled her eyes slightly. The blond girl smiled and sat down. The music teacher looked back down at her class list.

"Miss . . . Mailer, you're our newest member. Perhaps you can give us some insight into Beethoven's creative process."

Malory didn't respond at first.

"Miss Mailer?" Mrs. Lerner asked again, looking intently at Malory.

With a start Malory realized Mrs. Lerner was speaking to *her*.

"Well . . ." Malory hesitated.

It was an easy question for her. She'd read all about Beethoven. But she didn't want to seem like a show-off. Especially on her first day.

"We're waiting, Miss Mailer," Mrs. Lerner said, tapping her foot lightly on the cement floor, her head tilted expectantly to one side.

"Well, Beethoven wasn't born deaf." Malory spoke softly, the words tumbling out one after the other in a rush. "So he knew what the notes and instruments sounded like. And like most composers, he could hear the music in his head

34

first—before he wrote it down. Also, he would put his head on the piano when he played. That way he could feel the vibrations, and in his own way that's how he heard the music that ran through his head." When Malory was finished, she was sure she had said way too much.

There was an awed hush in the classroom. Malory could feel everyone's eyes on her. Mrs. Lerner smiled.

"Very good, Miss Mailer," she said quietly. "Very good."

Before she could say anything further, the bell rang. Music class was over. Malory breathed a sigh of relief. She'd gotten through the first day. Now all she had to do was ask Mrs. Lerner if there was a piano she could play.

Mrs. Lerner was collecting her lecture notes from the music stand as Malory approached her.

"Your answer was astute, Madeline," Mrs. Lerner said, looking up from her notes. "You spoke like someone who knows what she's talking about where composing music is concerned. Are you a musician?"

"I play the piano," she said shyly.

"Really? Are you interested in the orchestra?"

Malory nodded. "Maybe." She hesitated. "If I were in the orchestra, could I practice on the school piano?"

"You don't have one at home?" Mrs. Lerner asked.

"Well, um, no . . . at my old school I usually practiced on the piano there," Malory said, faltering over the lie.

"I see." Mrs. Lerner eyed her. "I'll tell you what. First things first. Let me listen to you play."

Malory followed her into the darkened auditorium adjacent to the music room.

"The one in here is somewhat better, although I must say neither is very good," Mrs. Lerner said as she flicked on the lights.

Malory breathed in the dusty auditorium smells. There it was—a grand piano to the side of the stage. Her eyes roved over it hungrily.

Mrs. Lerner unlocked and uncovered the piano, then she busied herself in the front row sorting out her pad, pen, and sheet music. Malory ran her hands over the smooth wood before sitting down.

Then she lifted the cover and put her slender fingers lightly on the cool, ivory keys. Bliss.

Mrs. Lerner cleared her throat loudly. "What are you going to play for me, Madeline?"

It didn't take Malory a second to decide. "Beethoven's *Sonata Pathétique*." This piece had been running through her head all week. "Um," she interrupted herself. "I was working on it before we moved, but I'm not quite finished, if that's all right with you."

"That's fine, dear."

Malory again touched her fingers to the keys. Then she closed her eyes and remembered where she had learned the Beethoven piece. Back at Lincoln Hills in a dusty practice room. In the hall outside, other kids laughed, yelled, and fooled around, making Malory feel more isolated than ever. Although Malory hadn't lived half the years of Beethoven, the piece made perfect sense to her. The melancholy . . . the isolation . . .

Malory lost all sense of time and place. It was just her and the music and the piano, weaving a story together, touching on every subtlety, rocking with emotion. . . .

As the last chord faded away, Malory slowly became aware of her surroundings again. Mrs. Lerner was watching her with a smile.

"Madeline, that was just lovely. Who did you say taught you back in . . ." She shuffled some papers to see where Malory had transferred from.

"Little Rock," Malory lied. "I had a bunch of teachers. No one for very long."

Mrs. Lerner took off her glasses. "You mean you've had no real musical education?"

Malory blushed. "Well, yes, that's true, I guess," she mumbled, shifting uncomfortably on the bench.

"That's remarkable," Mrs. Lerner said after a moment. She smiled wryly. "Actually I find that rather hard to believe, my dear."

Malory couldn't think of a response, so she just shrugged.

"And you say you have no piano. How on earth do you practice without a piano?"

Malory weighed her answer to this question. She was too embarrassed to admit that she practiced on a paper keyboard taped to the floor of her bedroom, imagining the sound of the notes, much as Beethoven had.

"I just practice whenever I can," she replied. Then she heard a faint noise up in the balcony. She jumped from the bench and quickly stood behind the piano.

Mrs. Lerner frowned. "Madeline, what's wrong?"

"Oh, nothing." Malory glanced into the balcony, then smiled and came out from behind the piano. "I guess it's just nerves . . . first day of school and all . . ." Her voice trailed off.

"Well, dear," Mrs. Lerner said, smiling warmly at her, "we would be quite proud to have you as part of our orchestra. There's only one problem."

Malory prepared herself for the inevitable—they had already promised the spot to someone else.

"I just think you'd be much happier on a better piano," Mrs. Lerner concluded. "As you can see, this one is all gloss and no substance."

Malory nodded, relief flooding through her.

She knew what Mrs. Lerner meant. The instrument had a tinny ring that no amount of tuning would fix.

"You can practice in the music room or here, whenever it's free," Mrs. Lerner continued, "but why don't you practice at my house once a week, say on Saturday afternoons? The piano is quite good."

Malory couldn't believe her ears. "Really? Oh, I'd love to . . . I mean, if it's okay. Well, you know what I mean."

"Yes, I think I do. It's settled, then. We can start this very Saturday, tomorrow. I live at 318 Baden Lane; I'll give you the directions. Say twelve noon?"

Malory was speechless. "That would be great," she finally managed.

Mrs. Lerner smiled broadly. "Good. Now let's lock up this old elephant and go home."

Three

WHEN MALORY ARRIVED home from
school, her mother's "new" car—an old
Dodge Dart—was parked out front. Mrs. Hunter
was back already from her first day as a book-
keeper for one of the local doctors.

Of all the apartments they'd lived in over the
years, Malory thought, this one was definitely the
worst. For starters, there was the location:
Crescent Drive was a cheesy little street that
started at the Unocal 76 gas station under
Interstate 10 and ended in a dead end, with a
view of an abandoned lot. Then there was the
building. Depressing, gray cinder block—and
only two floors of it. It was like a little jail,
Malory thought. There were seven other units in
the building, but the Hunters hadn't seen any of
their neighbors yet. Compared to the rest of west

L.A., the place was definitely a dump. Malory remembered that Jeffrey Laurence, the FBI agent who took the Hunters to their new apartment, had said, "It's not the most luxurious place."

"What a ridiculous understatement," Malory mumbled to herself.

As Malory entered the narrow hallway leading to their apartment she could smell what the other tenants were having for dinner—mostly fried food. The people right next door favored a deep-fried fish of some kind, and the landlord on the first floor clearly cooked his hamburgers in yesterday's grease. Down the hall someone was boiling cabbage and potatoes. The sour smells made Malory's nose crinkle.

She opened the door to 8J, the corner apartment, which directly faced the Unocal 76 in all its neon glory.

"Maddy, is that you?" her mother called from the living room, using her new, fake name. "Come on in here and tell me about your day."

Malory carefully avoided the kitchenette—a mere hallway with cracked linoleum and ridiculous "horn of plenty" wallpaper—and went into the living room. She dropped her bag on the floor.

"Hi, honey," Mrs. Hunter said as she put down her paperback—probably another Agatha Christie mystery, Malory thought—and made room on the couch for her. Mike and Tommy were sprawled in front of the TV, watching *X-Men,* with the remains of two bowls of cereal perilously close to their feet. Malory kissed them both on the heads. Their hair was now dyed a brown that was close to their natural shade. They both blissfully ignored her, laughing at the cartoon exploits. She was no match for *X-Men.* The twins were lucky, Malory often thought. They always had each other. Mike and Tommy were more or less content no matter what they were doing, as long as they were doing it together.

Malory's mother kissed her cheek and groaned as she got up from the couch. "Just a second, honey, I got you something." She went into her bedroom, just down the short hallway.

Malory lay down on the threadbare green couch and stared at the walls. They were an unusually ugly shade of beige. Or maybe they were once white, but the freeway fumes had stained it this lovely color. Malory grimaced.

Next to the old couch was an equally ancient orange stuffed easy chair and a plain, straight-backed chair. They faced a crummy old color TV on a shaky, pressed-wood stand. A musty-smelling braided rug finished the picture. One cruddy little window opened onto the street and the gas station.

Jeffrey said that the apartment was already furnished, but this is a sorry excuse for furniture, Malory thought glumly.

"Here you go, honey. Budge over." Malory's mom plopped down and handed her a plastic bag from The Gap.

"Oh, Mom." It was probably the guilt, Malory knew. Her mom always felt especially bad whenever they had to pick up and move. For maybe the millionth time Malory wondered: *What would it be like to have a normal life?*

Inside the bag were a pair of nice sand-washed jeans with slightly distressed knees—it must have killed her mom to buy predamaged clothes—and a cute white baby T-shirt.

"Great choice, Mom." Malory smiled.

"There's no doubt that things are tight around here, Mal, but I didn't think you could wait until you got a job for at least one change of clothes. Especially since it's like summer here." She checked her watch. "Tommy, honey, would you please turn to channel seven? The news is on."

Her mother and father were always watching the news—always. What were they looking for? Did they think there would be a fantastic break on the Carlotti crime family—that someday they would turn on the news and the announcer would say, "Hunters, if you can hear this, it is now safe to come home."

Malory shook her head. Home. She hardly remembered New York. She had been a little girl when they'd snuck off in the middle of the night into the waiting FBI sedan. For Malory, New

43

York meant the stoop of her building and her white canopied bed. That was all she could recall.

She sat back down on the couch and closed her eyes. As she had done so many times before, she recounted in her mind the events that had sentenced her family to a life of fear and constant moving.

Her father had been an accountant—not a terribly exciting job, but Malory remembered that he had always been proud of his work. He never saw himself as any kind of do-gooder, just a law-abiding citizen. All he had ever wanted was a normal, comfortable life for his family, in which he would work, raise his children, and take an occasional vacation.

One day at work he noticed that the books didn't add up. There were a lot of unexplained deposits. His coworker, Jimmy Moorhead, said that the numbers weren't adding up for him either. So the two of them started asking questions. Before long they were told in no uncertain terms to keep their mouths shut. That was when Mr. Hunter realized who he was working for—the Mafia. At that point he decided that his life and his family were more important than taking a stand, and he kept quiet. He planned to just get out and get another job.

But Jimmy wouldn't give up. He kept talking. And then he was killed—shot in the head in front of his own house. Once that happened,

Mr. Hunter knew that he had to speak up. He didn't want to put his family in danger, but he couldn't let this go without a fight. He didn't want his children to grow up in the shadow of his own fear.

Malory reminded herself that her father was just a decent, honest man who had tried to do the right thing. Even though she often blamed him, she knew that this whole mess wasn't his fault. The sad irony was that once he stood up for what was right, he had to hide for the rest of his life.

She leaned against the armrest of the couch and looked at her mother, who was watching TV. *She looks so tired,* Malory thought. Kathryn Hunter was only forty-four years old and definitely a pretty woman—but like the rest of the family, she had a pale, haunted look.

Now that Malory was older, it was clear where she got most of her looks. She and her mother both had the same full red lips and thin, straight noses. They were both slender, although Malory, at five-seven, was taller than her mother.

Looking at her mother now, it occurred to Malory that she had sacrificed a lot. Back in New York, her mother had been surrounded by family—brothers, sisters, cousins. Her parents were still alive. They had been a close, family-oriented, churchgoing group. Now Mrs. Hunter was cut off from her family and didn't belong to any church or organization. The only people she associated with regularly were her husband and children. Her mother suddenly glanced over at her, and Malory looked away. There was no way she could talk to her mother about all this. Once she had tried, and her mother had burst into tears. Malory had tried to comfort her—but it was a strange feeling, being like a parent to her mother.

"Hello, hello!"

Malory's father was home, acting too cheerful as usual. She could smell the Chinese takeout before she saw the bulging bag in his hands.

"You wouldn't believe what happened to me at work today," Mr. Hunter called as he walked into the kitchen. He always had a funny story from work. This one seemed to be about a contest between employees. Malory tried to pay attention. She knew she would have to make some kind of comment on it later. Her mother laughed as her father went on and on.

This is like some weird science fiction movie, Malory thought, *where everyone knows that the aliens are going to take over the earth, but they keep going about their business and pretending that everything's perfectly normal.*

". . . meanwhile," her father was saying, smiling widely with his arms full of Chinese food cartons, "José had made his display out of orange foods only! Hi, Maddy." He kissed her forehead. "Hi, Todd. Hi Mark!"

Malory's father always made a point of using their fake names. He tried to pretend it was like a fun game or something. None of them thought it was fun. She hated when he called her by a fake name.

"Hi, Daddy." Malory smiled up at him. *Even my smile is a fake,* she thought.

"I said, 'out of orange foods only!'" her father prompted them. "Where's my uproarious laughter? That's the end of the story!"

"It was very funny, Dad." Malory smiled again, hoping he'd drop it.

"Yeah, very funny, Dad." Mike tore into the beef and broccoli carton, eating with a fork. Tom used his chopstick skills to snag food from everyone else's plates. Malory smiled at him. Tom was the twin with the strange eating habits—they had even taken him to a doctor once when he had refused to eat anything but grapes for two whole weeks. In contrast, Mike ate everything and anything that was put in front of him. He once ate a whole plate of pork buns without noticing that he had eaten the paper on the bottom of each bun as well. "I *thought* it was kind of chewy," was all he had to say.

"So, Maddy," her father said, ignoring her reaction to the fake name, "tell us what your day was like today."

"There isn't much to tell," Malory said, sucking down a lo mein noodle. "I spent about a year looking for my classes, and I was practically trampled to death in the first five minutes. The whole place is full of socialites, and nobody except for this one guy even noticed I was alive. . . ."

Her parents nodded sympathetically.

"First days are always hard," her mother said.

"Very overwhelming," her father murmured in agreement.

Malory wanted to scream. Sometimes her parents tried so hard to be understanding that it drove her crazy. How was she supposed to grow up and rebel against parents who sympathized about everything? Especially since it was all *their* fault that everything was so hard?

She sighed. The whole thing wasn't normal, and it probably never would be.

She reviewed her day in her mind. At least tutoring was something to look forward to—it was a way for her to make money *and* reach out to other people from her isolated world.

"I also went by the job board," she continued. "I'm tutoring this kid named Joey Pataki. I met him; he's a cute kid—"

Mike frowned.

"No, not as cute as you." She took a bite of broccoli. "Anyway, the best part of the day was music appreciation. The music teacher, Mrs. Lerner, says I can be in orchestra." Malory smiled triumphantly. "I can practice at her house on Saturdays, and I got a whole pile of new music!"

"That's great, honey," her father said quietly.

"Sounds like fun," Malory's mother quickly added.

Malory knew what they were really thinking. It was too dangerous for her to join any clubs or after-school activities. It was especially dangerous for her to join the orchestra, since she was such a talented musician. She always stuck out like a sore thumb in any high-school band. But they didn't have the heart to tell her she couldn't have the one thing that mattered most to her, especially when she had so little else.

"Do they have practice rooms at the school?" Malory's mother asked brightly. "I bet they do. Why don't you ask your music teacher about it, and I'm sure . . ."

"That's a good idea," continued her father. "I know that most musicians need a lot of privacy, and—"

Malory couldn't take it anymore. If her music endangered them all, it was a responsibility she didn't want.

"If you don't want me to play the piano," Malory started quietly, trying to control her temper, "I'll tell Mrs. Lerner I can't play, I'll take back the music, and we'll all be safe and sound in our cozy little jail cell here."

Her parents stared at her in silence.

Malory got up from the table, trying not to appear too upset so that she wouldn't disturb the twins. "Excuse me," she said quietly, "I have homework to do." And with that she rushed from the room.

"Mal . . ." Her father started, but his voice was silenced as she slammed the door of her tiny bedroom shut.

Just leave me alone, she pleaded silently as she flopped down on her bed. She closed her eyes; the beige walls seemed to be closing in. This place really *was* a jail. There was no difference. She wondered what her parents' muffled voices were really saying. After a few moments there was a quiet knocking on her door.

"Come in," she grumbled.

Malory avoided her father's eyes as he perched himself on the edge of the mattress.

"Mal, I know this is hard," her father began.

"What do you mean?" she asked reluctantly.

"I mean . . . well, for one thing, you've taken on more than your share of responsibility in this family."

Malory remained silent.

"And I know you've had to grow up faster than a lot of kids your age."

"In some ways, yeah, I guess." Malory shifted uncomfortably. What was he going to do? Give her back the last eleven years? Why didn't he just drop it?

"This isn't how I had pictured you growing up, not at all." His voice was strained.

"I know," she said.

"I had always seen you as being one of those well-adjusted city girls." He cleared his throat and forced a smile. "The kind who comes home after school and sees her friends and has lots of activities and dates, and who also enjoys all the things a big city has to offer. Concerts, museums, whatever."

"Yeah . . . that sounds great," Malory said dully.

"Nobody's perfect, Malory. Especially the FBI."

"Tell me about it," she said, feeling anger well within her again. "If I hadn't noticed that New York license plate in Lincoln Hills . . ." She didn't finish the sentence.

"Let's just be thankful you did," her father said. "You know, it was really something the way you picked up the boys and got us out of town before those men even knew what was happening. I'm very proud of you."

"Yeah, well, I've had a lot of practice," Malory said flatly.

"Maddy—Malory, honey, look—" he began.

"Forget it, Dad. Don't worry about it. I'll be fine," Malory said. Her voice grew strained.

Mr. Hunter was silent. His body sagged. He got up to go. "You know, Mal, the FBI says this won't go on forever."

"Yeah, and their information has always been so reliable," Malory snapped. She was immediately sorry she'd said it when she saw how her father winced.

"No, you're right, Mal," he said, pausing at her door. "They haven't been too reliable. It's been six moves now in eleven years, and you have every right to be mad—at me, at them. But I couldn't live with myself if I didn't do what I did back in New York. I know the Carlottis are still in business—and I don't know any better way to keep us safe. And neither does the FBI."

"I know, Dad. I know. I'm sorry."

He shook his head. "Don't be. I guess I am being too paranoid. I don't want you to feel scared all the time. Just make sure you blend in— don't call attention to yourself. No pictures, no photos—just be part of the scenery." He glanced at her newly blackened hair and grinned ruefully. "Do your best to keep a low profile, Snow White."

Mr. Hunter closed the door behind him.

Malory lay back against the lumpy mattress. She was exhausted. A million different thoughts buzzed around her brain. Maybe it was true. Maybe this wouldn't go on forever. Maybe then they could go back to New York and live like a normal family, in the beautiful brownstone with the white canopied bed. . . .

Or maybe not.

Malory looked out her bedroom window out at the ugly grate of the fire escape. The neon Unocal 76 sign flashed across her face. L.A. was a big place. Millions of people drove through it every day. They were safe. For now.

Weren't they?

Malory wondered what Ben was doing tonight. Whatever it was, he was probably surrounded by beautiful girls with no problems and great clothes.

Malory shook her head, determined to keep Ben out of her mind. She knew her father was right. The important thing was to keep a low profile—to keep the family as safe as possible. Long ago she had promised herself she'd do anything, give up anything to make sure that she, her parents, and her brothers were safe.

Resolved to do just that, Malory closed her eyes and willed herself to sleep.

Four

MALORY WOKE UP early on Saturday morning. The glowing red numbers of her digital clock read 8:03. *Too early,* she said to herself, and closed her eyes again. But she couldn't go back to sleep. After a few minutes of tossing and turning, she got up and went into the bathroom to brush her teeth.

She studied her reflection in the bathroom mirror. She was getting used to her jet-black hair. The first few days of assuming a new identity were always weird. She had to get used to a new look and a new name—as well as remember the new names for her brothers and parents. It was a strain.

Sighing, Malory jumped into the shower. The pulsing hot water relaxed her, and she thought about going back to bed—but she knew she wouldn't be able to fall asleep. Instead she pulled on the new sand-washed jeans and T-shirt her mother had given her. Now she felt just a little bit less like an outsider. At least she didn't look like a cold-weather refugee anymore.

Malory's dad had already left for his weekend job at an Italian restaurant just over in Santa Monica. Jeffrey Laurence had set him up as the weekend manager of the restaurant. Mr. Hunter didn't have much experience with restaurants, but he was a fast learner. The witness protection program had forced him to become a master of all trades, as he took on a different job every time the Hunters moved.

Frankly, his absence was a huge relief. The apartment was just too small for the five of them. Besides, Malory always felt like she had to be "Maddy" when her father was around. It was almost as bad as being at school.

Malory walked out of her room in her old hiking boots and started for the door. Mike and Tommy were watching *Gladiators 2000,* and Malory easily snuck by the living room without distracting them. Now if only her mother wasn't in the kitchen . . .

"Aren't you the early riser," Mrs. Hunter remarked. She was hunched over the stove, making scrambled eggs. "Hungry?"

Malory looked down at the cracked, stained

linoleum. This place was such a dump. "No thanks, Mom," she mumbled.

"You sleep all right?" her mother asked.

"Yeah . . . I guess I'm just excited about playing the piano at Mrs. Lerner's."

Her mother smiled. "I'll bet you are, sweetie."

Mrs. Hunter seemed especially cheerful that morning. Malory knew that meant she was more worried than usual—but Malory decided it would be wise to keep her thoughts to herself. She started to help her mother by setting the kitchen table, humming softly her favorite de Falla concertino.

"I always liked that piece," Mrs. Hunter said wistfully. "And you play it so beautifully. It's my favorite," she added.

"Really?" Malory asked. She was surprised that her mother even remembered. "I guess it's my favorite too."

Malory's mother looked away. She began stirring the eggs furiously. "When this is all over, Mal, you're going to have a normal life. A piano at home, friends, boyfriends . . . everything."

For a moment Malory held her breath. She didn't want to start the morning like this, with guilt and empty promises and false hopes. But she knew her mother was only doing the best she could.

"A piano at home, friends, a boyfriend . . ."

Try none of the above, Malory thought, letting her anger get the best of her. But for some reason the image of Ben's face popped into her mind. She supposed *he* was about the closest thing to a friend that she had—and she had barely exchanged a dozen sentences with him. But he did seem nice. He also seemed eager to get to know her. And he was undeniably cute. . . .

Just then the harsh sound of the phone ringing disrupted her thoughts. Her pulse quickened. She glanced at her mother. Mrs. Hunter's eyes were wide—and Malory knew the reason.

Their number was unlisted.

Without hesitating, Mrs. Hunter picked up the phone from its cradle on the wall of the kitchen.

"Hello," she said evenly.

Could it be Dad? Malory wondered. Maybe he had gotten lost on the way to work.

"Hello?" Mrs. Hunter repeated, a little more forcefully. She stared at the phone for a few seconds, then frowned and hung up. "Must have been a wrong number," she muttered.

Malory swallowed. "Must have been."

In a brisk voice that belied her worry, Mrs. Hunter said, "Well, let's eat so we can get on with our day."

With the wind rushing through her hair and the bright California sunshine beating down on her, Malory almost managed to forget about how much she hated her new home.

The bike ride to Mrs. Lerner's house would probably have only taken about fifteen minutes, but Malory had chosen to leave the house early and take a long, circuitous route—mostly to escape. After breakfast her mother had charged her with keeping an eye on the twins while she went shopping. Malory didn't mind the responsibility, but the depression of being in that apartment—coupled with the worry of the mysterious phone call—had made her tense and irritable. As soon as her mother had returned with the groceries, Malory had hopped on her bike.

But now she was feeling much better. This area of Los Angeles was particularly good for biking—flat and tree lined and spacious, with little traffic. If she could ride her bike a lot, she might actually get used to this place, she realized. A couple of high-school boys passed her on the sidewalk, headed in the other direction, and Malory found herself studying their faces. She shook her head. As silly as it was, she'd been secretly hoping to run into Ben. What were the chances of that—in a city of eight million? This wasn't Lincoln Hills, after all.

Before she knew it, she was turning onto Baden Lane. She couldn't help but notice how much nicer this block was than her own: There were ranch houses with wide green lawns and white fences; everything had a quiet, cared-for look about it. Malory glanced at the numbers: 314, 316 . . . *there.*

Three Hundred and Eighteen Baden Lane was a small home with a yellow quarry-stone facing. Purple, pink, and white flowers bordered the small walkway to the steps. Malory felt a twinge of sadness as she parked her bike and walked up to the front door. The lawn, the basketball hoop over the garage, the skateboard leaning against the garage door—it all looked as if it had always been there and always would. *Things are permanent here,* she said to herself. *And permanence is something I know nothing about.*

"Hello, is anybody home?" she called in through the front screen door.

"Hello?" Malory called again, pressing her face to the screen. Inside it was cool and dark.

"Hello, Madeline!"

Malory jumped. Behind her was Mrs. Lerner, rooting through a big purse and looking harried. "I have to run off—I won't be back for a while. I can't find the spare keys. My husband and son will be home at some point. Oh, you can just leave it unlocked; it'll be fine. I left some music by the piano for you. Have a good time!" And with that, she raced down the driveway.

Malory smiled and shook her head.

Entering the house, Malory stood in the slate-floored hallway and noticed how everything had a place. To the right of the entranceway was the family room. It looked so cozy with its soft brown leather couch and love seat, positioned around a large square mosaic coffee table. The couches faced a big-screen TV along the wall. An entertainment center crowded with books and games and videotapes surrounded the TV.

To the left of the hallway was the living room. Nestled in a corner of the oversize room, just far enough from the stone fireplace, was a beautiful, cherry wood, baby grand piano. The sunlight that filtered in from the white-curtained picture windows gave the room a feeling of spaciousness and peace at the same time.

Permanence, Malory said to herself again, painfully envious that people could live such normal, ordinary lives. For a moment she wished with all her heart that she could be a part of Mrs. Lerner's family instead of her own.

She walked over to the piano and carefully, almost tenderly sifted through the pages of music that Mrs. Lerner had taken out for her. Most of her favorite pieces were there, including the concertina she'd been humming at breakfast. She spread it out on the music stand and lifted the cover from the keys.

Ever since she was little, everyone had always

told her that she was a prodigy. Malory knew she had a gift. She had been pounding on the used upright piano in the hall in the family's brownstone since she was old enough to sit up on her own and had worked up to Christmas carols by the time she was four. At five she had started on the intermediate player books—and had even won a prize at her first recital for her rendition of "Once There Were Three Fishermen." As if that hadn't been enough, she had informed her teacher that the piece was actually an étude written by Ludwig van Beethoven.

Slowly, unselfconsciously she put her fingers to the piano, and within seconds her mind was far away. As always Malory let the music flood through her, taking her to a long-forgotten place where she was Malory Hunter, not Maddy Mailer or some other stupid name that had nothing to do with her.

As Malory played, her face glowed—and the rich tones of the piano vibrated through her body. She swayed on the bench, moved by the rhythm of the concertina. Her nimble fingers happily danced on the keys. Midway through the piece, on familiar ground, Malory closed her eyes, remembering the music in her heart, not needing the written notes any longer.

Time ceased to exist. For what seemed like hours Malory played piece after piece—some from the music Mrs. Lerner had left for her but mostly from memory. And as she played, the pain of her isolation subsided just a little.

In the midst of a particularly lyrical passage the image of Ben's wide grin popped suddenly into Malory's head. This part of the piece had always sounded like laughter to her—and for some reason her unconscious mind had associated it with the only other thing that could make her laugh at this point in her life: some boy whom she hardly knew.

Finally her hands came down in unison on the final chord. Her eyes remained closed as she let the harmony engulf her and then fade into silence.

A burst of loud clapping made her jump.

Malory's eyes flew open. Her heart was pounding, and her lashes fluttered in disbelief. She wasn't alone. Slowly she took her hands from the keys and sat there, frozen, gazing at the shadowy figure in the corner of the room.

"Don't stop," the figure said quietly.

And then she knew who it was.

"Ben?" Malory gasped. "What—what are *you* doing here?"

"Well, for starters," Ben said, stepping out of the shadows, "I live here. And you?" he added with a grin.

"You—you live *here?*" Malory stood up so suddenly that she almost knocked over the piano bench.

"Hard to believe, isn't it?" Ben asked with good-natured sarcasm. "I know it's not much— but it's home. Let me guess. You must be the special student my mother was expecting."

Suddenly it all fell into place. Ben was Mrs. Lerner's *son*. Malory took in his wind-tousled brown hair, his clear dark brown eyes, and the reddened patches of sunburn that smudged the top of his cheekbones. Yes, now that she knew, she could definitely see the similarity between Ben and his mom. But still, it was just so . . . *strange*.

"I'm sorry if I bothered you," he said.

Malory shook her head. "You didn't." She peered at him closely. His hands were behind his back, as if he were hiding something. "What do you have there . . . ?"

"I hope you don't mind," he said suddenly, revealing a sketch pad.

Malory gasped with surprise.

She found that she was staring at *herself*. It was an exact reproduction: she was at the piano, her slender hands in motion. The pencil-drawn figure appeared to be playing in a dreamlike trance, surrounded by a hazy pool of light.

"That's me," she whispered incredulously. "How did you do that?"

Ben shrugged. "It's nothing. I mean, I do it all the time," he added, perhaps as an explanation for why he was so good at it. "You were sitting

63

there for so long, I just couldn't resist. . . ."

"It's really something," Malory said. She looked up into Ben's eyes admiringly.

"Thanks," Ben said. He quickly averted his gaze, as if he were embarrassed. "Actually, I've been thinking about sketching you from the first moment I saw you. And when I saw that you were here in my living room, you know, uh, I just had to make the most of the opportunity. . . ."

At that moment Malory's heart froze.

What was she thinking? She couldn't have sketches of her floating around town, not even in Ben's sketch notebook. What if someone got hold of them? The *wrong* someone?

Malory's father's voice echoed resoundingly in her head: *"No pictures, no photos."*

"I kind of wish you hadn't done that," Malory found herself saying.

Ben looked up, a startled expression on his face. "What do you mean?"

"You know, you really shouldn't draw someone unless you ask her permission first," Malory said nervously. She knew Ben must think she was acting weird, but she couldn't do anything about it.

"Well, I didn't—didn't think you'd mind . . . ," Ben stammered.

"I do mind," she said—perhaps a little more harshly than she'd intended. "And in fact, I'll have to ask you to give me that sketch, if *you* don't mind." Malory held out her hand expectantly.

"Fine," Ben retorted. His tone was brusque. He tore the page from his notebook and handed it to her. "I would have given it to you anyway, if I knew you'd wanted it," he muttered, closing the pad and putting away his pencils.

Malory wanted to say something—*anything*—to explain herself, but all she could do was stare at the hurt in Ben's eyes. There was no way he could have any clue of what was going on with her. She longed to tell him why she couldn't be sketched. She knew if she told him the real reason, he would be sympathetic and understanding. He might even take her in his arms and comfort her. The very thought made her heart race. She looked over at him, still fiddling with the pad and his pencils.

But Malory couldn't tell Ben. Not now. Not ever. Not for his sake, and not for the sake of her family and their safety. In her heart Malory knew it was better to just cut the cord completely, right here and right now.

She looked at the sketch in her hands. Her fingers were shaking.

Then she felt Ben's eyes on her, burning into her. Malory knew she should tear the sketch to pieces, but she couldn't bring herself to do it.

I'll get rid of it later, she thought.

She rolled it up quickly and stuffed it into her pack. Then she all but ran for the front door.

"Tell your mom thanks, please, and . . ."

Malory looked back over her shoulder. "Uh . . . I'll see you at school."

She had caught a brief glimpse of Ben's crest-fallen face as she turned away from him. Before she knew what was happening, tears were welling in her eyes.

"Hey, Maddy—wait!" Ben called.

She hesitated as he came up behind her.

"Look, you were right," Ben said. His voice was pleading, no longer angry.

"Don't worry about it," she breathed.

Now I won't ever be able to come back here, she told herself bitterly. *Not to play the beautiful piano, because Ben will be here.* He surely would never want to speak to or see her again after the way she'd acted. And she couldn't blame him. In a way, that had been her intention, hadn't it?

It wasn't until then that Malory realized how much she'd been hoping that she and Ben could be . . . well, at least friends.

Forget about that, she thought miserably.

Without another word she bolted out the door.

Five

B Y THE TIME Malory had to go to the library to meet Joey Pataki—the ten-year-old boy whom she was supposed to tutor—some of the embarrassment and remorse had subsided. It had been almost two hours since she'd left the Lerners', and she'd spent that time biking around some more, working out her frustrations. She should have never even talked to Ben in the first place, she realized. She should never talk to anyone her age, period. Silence would keep her from getting hurt.

It was nearly five o'clock. Her legs were beginning to ache, but at least she was in a better mood. She turned onto the broad avenue that led to the library.

But as she started coasting down the hill, Malory got the all-too-familiar sense that she was being followed.

Automatically she rode out of the bike lane and onto the sidewalk, slowing to a halt. There she fiddled with her backpack, pretending to adjust the straps, while she watched the cars go by out of the corner of her eye.

A black Jeep Cherokee with shaded windows drove slowly along the side of the street where Malory stood.

She held her breath. Her heart knocked painfully against her ribs.

Don't panic. Just start pedaling, nice and easy. Don't look at the car. Whatever you do, don't look at the car. . . .

The Jeep slowed to a stop and pulled up alongside her. The tinted window rolled down.

Malory gripped the handlebars so hard that her knuckles were white. She quickly twisted the bike around and sat up on the pedals, about to push off, when she heard a voice say, "How about a lift?"

She jerked the bike to a halt. She knew that voice.

"I—I . . . ," she stammered, then closed her mouth. Ben was sitting in the driver's seat. She just glared at him, not knowing whether to feel happy, relieved, ashamed, or annoyed.

"Are you all right?" Ben asked, leaning over and sticking his head through the window. He looked concerned.

"Yeah, sure, I'm fine," Malory answered faintly, trying to recover.

"Want a ride home? That way I can apologize for drawing you and ask your permission for next time."

Malory bit her lip. Why was he being so sweet? Couldn't he see that it wouldn't get him anywhere?

"Well, I'm not going home yet," she said carefully.

"How about a ride to wherever you're going, then?" Ben asked with a grin.

"Uh, I'm going to the library," she said. "It's not that far—"

"The library?" he interrupted. "What a coincidence. I'm going in that direction."

Without waiting for Malory to protest further, Ben jumped out of the car, lifted her bicycle into the back, and opened the passenger side door with a gentlemanly sweep of his hand.

"You don't take no for an answer, do you?" she mumbled, climbing into the passenger side, but she couldn't help but smile.

"Nope." He jumped in on the other side and started the engine. Then he turned to her and put his hand lightly on hers. "You know, I'm sorry about the sketch. And I didn't mean to sneak up on you. I just didn't want to bother you. You looked so . . . happy."

Malory look down at Ben's fingers, smudged black with pencil and charcoal. She couldn't help but feel an electric tingle of excitement as his skin

69

touched hers. But he was looking at her with a relaxed, friendly expression. Was it just an apologetic gesture? Or did he mean something more?

"Will you forgive me?" he prodded.

She nodded, looking up into his large brown eyes. For a moment she forgot they were sitting in his car by the side of the road. Right then Malory felt as she did when she played the piano—floating, safe and free. Without meaning to, she smiled happily.

A car horn blared loudly behind them, breaking the spell. Malory jumped. They both laughed, then Ben put his hands on the wheel and stepped on the gas. The connection was broken.

"Look, Ben, I'm sorry I freaked out. I—I just . . ." Malory stopped. She didn't want to lie to him. But she couldn't tell him the truth either.

"Forget about it," Ben said, keeping his eyes on the road. "It's okay, really. I understand."

Malory sighed, and they rode the rest of the way in silence. When they reached the library, Ben got Malory's bike out of the back and helped her chain it to the bike rack. For the second time in less than five minutes Malory wondered, *Why is he being so kind to me?* But then she just figured that was probably the way he was naturally. With everyone.

"Uh . . . that was nice," she said once the bike was all locked up.

He gave her a confused smile.

"I mean the ride," she added hastily. "Thanks a lot."

"No problem," he said. "I was on my way here anyway."

Malory looked at the ground in the awkward silence that followed.

"I mean . . . uh, around here. I'm supposed to meet Seth and some of the guys at the CD store down the road," Ben said, glancing at the library's big double doors. "I'll walk you in."

She smiled. "Thanks." She could feel herself starting to blush, so she quickly began walking toward the entrance. "I'm meeting someone here."

Ben gave Malory a quick sidelong glance as he held open one of the doors for her. "A hot date, huh?" he asked, cocking an eyebrow.

Malory looked at him again. She couldn't tell if he sounded jealous—or if he was just teasing her, the way an older brother would tease a younger sibling. "You might say that," she said.

His face fell. Malory couldn't help but feel a strange relief. He wouldn't have been disappointed if he was just teasing her.

He sighed. "Well, I guess I'll—"

"Madeline!" a high-pitched voice called from the library floor.

"And there he is now," Malory said.

Joey Pataki definitely stood out in a library. He looked as if he belonged on a playground—and nowhere else. His grubby T-shirt hung loosely from his small, wiry body, and his blond hair was rumpled, sticking out in all directions. He waved at her excitedly. A few people at tables nearby were starting to frown at him.

Ben stared at Joey. Then he started to laugh.

"Be quiet!" someone hissed.

"Over here, Madeline!" Joey yelled.

"Shhh!" someone else whispered fiercely.

Malory glanced at Ben, and suddenly she burst into hysterical laughter.

"I'll be right back," she said, vainly trying to gain control of herself. "I gotta make sure he doesn't yell again. Last time I saw him, he was wild the whole time." She hurried over to the table where Joey was sitting and knelt beside him.

"What's so funny?" Joey whispered.

"Nothing, nothing," Malory whispered back, trying to ignore the angry stares of those around her. "Listen, I'm just going to say good-bye to my friend, and then I'll be right back, okay?"

Joey nodded. "Okay."

Madeline quickly followed Ben back outside, where she promptly started giggling again.

"I could learn a thing or two from that kid," Ben said wryly. "He really knows how to get someone's attention. Is he your little brother?"

Malory shook her head. Tears had started to form in her eyes from laughing so hard.

"No—he's just a boy I'm supposed to tutor."

Ben smiled, looking impressed. "So not only are you an amazing piano player, you're also a tutor," he said. "Wow. What else do you do? Run marathons?"

At the mention of the word *run,* the last bit of laughter died in Malory's throat. She lowered her head. *I don't run marathons—but I do run. I'm running right now.*

Benjamin looked puzzled. "Hey—are you okay? I didn't offend you or anything, did I?"

She drew in her breath sharply. "No, it's just . . ." She let the sentence hang. *It's just that I can never be honest with you.* She glanced at the door. "I should really go back in there," she breathed.

"Look," Ben said quickly. "I'd like to see you again. You know, we can just hang out. I don't have to sketch you or anything—"

"The sketch thing was my fault," she interrupted. "I didn't mean to be so rude about it—"

"So is that a yes?" Ben cut in, arching his eyebrows hopefully.

Malory didn't know what to say. She kept her eyes pinned to the ground. Part of her wanted to hang out with Ben more than anything in the world. But the other part was scared—of answering questions, of getting too close . . . of getting hurt.

Just then Joey's round face peeked through

the library doors. "Hey, Madeline—are you coming?" he called.

She looked at Joey—then back at Ben. Ben's expectant face demanded she make a decision.

"I'd like to hang out," she found herself saying quietly.

"Great!" Ben exclaimed. "How about when you're done here?"

A smile spread across her face. He certainly didn't waste any time.

"I'll pick you up in, like, an hour?" he asked.

She nodded. "Sure. That would be nice."

"Okay," he said happily. "I'll see you then. Bye, Maddy."

Malory watched as he hopped back into the Jeep and roared off down the avenue. A dizzying mix of euphoria and despair coursed through her. *What have I done?* she thought desperately. She shouldn't be getting together with him. She was leading him on. There could never be anything between them.

He doesn't even know my real name.

Six

"HOW ABOUT MY house?" Ben suggested as he put Malory's bike back into his car. "My parents won't mind."

Malory shook her head as she climbed into the Jeep. Dusk had begun to fall in the hour that she had been inside the library, and she was tired. She knew if Mrs. Lerner were there, she would ask all kinds of questions about Malory's musical background—and Malory would have to keep up a steady stream of lies. She just didn't have the energy for that right now. Joey Pataki had done a pretty good job of wearing her out.

"Then how about your house?" Ben asked.

"Definitely not!" She winced at the shrill, forceful sound of her own voice. *Great,* she thought miserably. *That didn't sound suspicious in the least.*

Ben blinked. "Well, okay," he said slowly.

Malory gave him a weak smile.

"How about pizza?" Ben asked. His tone was casual. "We can go to Alonzo's. It's right off Highland Avenue."

"Sure," she said, ready to agree to anything at this point. "That sounds good."

"Great." Ben grinned. "It's not far."

Malory stared out the open window as he pulled into traffic. The sun was a fiery red ball on the horizon, and a cool breeze ruffled her hair. She allowed herself a smile. Was this what it was like to feel normal? Going to have pizza with a boy on a beautiful Saturday night?

"So how was your hot date?" Ben asked after a moment.

Malory laughed. "Good," she replied. "Joey's a really bright kid, actually. The only problem is he can't sit still long enough to concentrate on anything."

Ben nodded. "Hmmm. I can relate to that."

"Really?" Malory turned and stole a quick peek at him. He was navigating through the busy street with a thoughtful, intense expression. "You strike me as the type who can sit still for a really long time."

"Only when I'm drawing," he said in a far-away voice. He turned to her and smiled. "Or in the company of someone interesting."

Malory quickly shifted her gaze back out the

window. Her mind was whirling confusedly. One minute talking to Ben seemed like the easiest thing in the world. The next minute she got so flustered, she couldn't even form a coherent sentence. Especially when he looked at her with those big brown eyes.

"So where do you live?" he asked.

Uh-oh. "Oh, in an apartment building not too far from here," she said dismissively. "You know, you've got a great house," she said, hoping to talk about something—*anything*—other than her own life.

He laughed once. "You think?"

"Yeah. It's like it's been there forever."

"And ever and ever," Ben said dully. He shrugged. "I guess I'm just bored with it. I've been there my whole life. But thanks anyway." He pulled to a stop at a red light and looked at her. "Now tell me about all the places you've been and let me live vicariously through you," he said, grinning.

Malory swallowed. She kept her eyes fixed to the stoplight. "Oh, I've never gone anywhere good, just small towns." The words tumbled out of her mouth in a rush. She had to shift the conversation away from herself and back to Ben. "So what kind of pizza do you want to—"

"Come on, Maddy," he interrupted gently. "You had to have been *somewhere* interesting."

"Nope." Her voice was flat. "Nowhere."

The light turned green, and the car lurched forward. "Well, name one place. Let me decide."

Malory found herself getting angry, even though she was well aware she had no right to be. It was the most ridiculous thing in the world. Ben was just curious about her—naturally and rightfully so. "Oak Bluffs, Iowa," she lied.

"Really!" he exclaimed with exaggerated excitement. "That sounds *amazing!*"

Malory laughed.

"Hey—is it true that in small towns everyone knows you by name?" Ben asked.

"Um, I guess for some people," she mumbled.

"Not for you, huh?"

Malory shook her head bitterly. "No way."

"I'd like that," he stated, apparently oblivious to the odd hardness in her tone. "I'd like to be somewhere where no one knows me. Someplace far away. Someplace where they don't even speak English."

Malory stared at him in disbelief. "Are you serious?" she asked. It seemed like such a luxury to her to have his kind of life. She practically ached with envy.

He raised his shoulders slightly. "Yeah. Actually I'd love to go to Vienna one day."

"How come?"

"Well, I have a great-aunt and great-uncle there. Vienna would be a really amazing place to paint. But let's talk about something more important. Pepperoni and mushroom sound good to you?"

Malory wiped her greasy fingers on a napkin, then leaned back in the big stuffed seat in the booth and sighed contentedly.

Ben smiled across the table at her. "Ready for another pie?"

"Are you serious?" she said with a laugh. "I couldn't eat another slice!"

"Well, I guess I could make do with the rest of your crusts," Ben said, surveying her plate.

Malory nodded, and Ben eagerly began munching on her discarded crusts. A small smile played on her lips. He was so cute when he ate— like a little boy, almost. It contrasted sharply with the rest of his personality, which struck her as mature beyond his seventeen years.

At least he hadn't asked any more personal questions, she reflected gratefully. He must have gotten the picture. They'd spent the entire dinner discussing Los Angeles—and all the lame people at her new school. Apparently she'd been right: Ben hated Shella and the rest of the Bubblehead set—but they wouldn't leave him alone. Ben was good friends with Seth and a couple of other guys, but he enjoyed spending time alone more than hanging out with the guys.

He's an outsider, just like me, she realized. *Maybe that's why it's so easy for us to talk to each other.*

"You sure you don't want anything else?" he mumbled with his mouth full.

"No," said Malory, looking out the floor-to-ceiling window. The sun had already sunk far below the horizon. "I told my mom I'd be home before dark, and I'm really going to have to motor if I'm going to make it."

"How about giving her a call and telling her we're going to a movie instead?" Ben asked.

Malory's heart gave a little jump. Pizza in the early evening was one thing. She'd had pizza with guys before—not often, but once or twice. But pizza and a movie? That definitely qualified as "date" material. She'd never been on a real date in her whole life. She bit her lip. She couldn't go out on a date with Ben, at least not tonight. Her parents had probably already begun to panic. She needed to get home.

"I mean, you know, if you're not busy or any-thing," Ben added. His confident tone faltered for a moment.

Malory was quiet. She reached out her hand and lightly placed it on Ben's arm. The smooth skin was warm. It felt so good just to *touch* him. His eyes widened hopefully.

"Ben, I don't think . . . ," Malory began in an apologetic way.

"Hey, that's okay," Ben said, immediately moving his arm out from under her fingers. He reached into his pocket and threw a wad of bills on the table. "Some other time. It's hot in here. Let's blow this joint." He stood up quickly from his seat, then snaked his way between the crowded close-together tables, heading for the door.

"Ben . . . ," Malory called. She chased him into the cool twilight air.

"Look, we better get you home before it's really dark," Ben said matter-of-factly. "I don't want your mom to worry."

Malory shifted awkwardly on her feet, trying to meet his gaze, but he kept looking away. She felt sick knowing that she had hurt his feelings. Wasn't there some way she could demonstrate that she really, truly *wanted* to spend more time with him? "You don't have to drive," she said timidly. "I can bike home."

He looked up at her sharply. Anger seemed to flare in his eyes for a moment. But then all at once his gaze softened.

"Just because you won't go to the movies with me, I'm not going to just leave you here," he said. "I would never do that."

Malory nodded. It was true; she knew it without his having to tell her. Ben would never do something like that. Ben would never do anything to hurt anyone on purpose.

He smiled. "Come on, I'll take you home."

They began walking toward the Jeep in silence, side by side. Suddenly she realized how she could show Ben that she wasn't blowing him off.

Her pulse picked up a beat. She could show him that she'd had a wonderful time—and that she'd like to see him again soon. And best of all, she wouldn't even have to open her mouth.

She reached over and took Ben's hand.

Ben didn't acknowledge the gesture by smiling at her, or acting nervous, or slowing his pace. He didn't even turn in her direction. He simply squeezed her hand gently, then let his fingers intertwine with hers.

Malory sighed. The Jeep was only a few feet farther. She wished that it wasn't there at all, that they could just keep walking like this forever, hand in hand. . . .

Ben slipped his fingers from hers and unlocked the doors.

"I had a nice time tonight," she said quietly as she climbed in.

Ben nodded. "Me too." He started up the engine and pulled onto the street, then turned on the radio. For some reason he kept flipping through the stations, without stopping at any particular one for more than two seconds.

"What are you looking for?" Malory finally asked.

"Uh, a classical station," Ben admitted sheepishly. "I don't usually listen to classical, but since you're in the car . . ."

Malory smiled. "Hey, I do listen to music

from the twentieth century," she said. "I even *play* music from the twentieth century."

"Whew," Ben said. He let the dial stop on an alternative rock station.

For the rest of the ride they listened to the radio. Malory gazed out the tinted window of the Jeep. The magic of the short time they'd held hands was starting to fade. Now she was wondering how she was going to get Ben to just leave without coming up to her apartment.

After seeing *his* house, she definitely didn't want him seeing the inside of that sad-looking dump. And she didn't want to have to explain about Ben to her mother and then to Mike and Tommy.

The Jeep pulled up slowly beside the curb in front of the apartment house.

"Well, here we are," Malory said brightly, hopping out the door the moment the car stopped. "I'll get the bike out."

Ben just laughed. "Don't worry. I'll get it out."

Out of habit Malory gave the street a once-over glance while Ben was removing the bike, just to see if anyone suspicious was hanging around. But the streets were empty, not a soul in sight—although an occasional car whizzed past them.

"Here you go," Ben said.

"Thanks," Malory said, taking her bike

from him. "And thanks for the ride and the pizza."

"Want me to walk you up?" he asked.

"No, thanks, I'll be fine," Malory assured him quickly.

"Are you sure?" Ben asked, glancing dubiously at the ugly, darkened apartment complex, where a lone bulb lit the entranceway. "You know, I don't mind."

Malory just stared at him. "No, it's . . ." She didn't finish. She didn't even know what she was trying to say.

Ben smiled sadly. The expression on his face seemed to beckon to her—the big eyes and full, soft lips. She found herself leaning close to him.

He took a step toward her.

Malory held her breath. She was afraid Ben could hear her heart thumping against her ribs. She wanted Ben to kiss her. To hold her against him. She wanted to reach up and put her arms around his neck and to feel a handful of his thick, soft brown hair run through her fingers. She suddenly realized she was gripping the handlebars of her bike so tightly that her hands ached.

He bent over and planted a delicate kiss on her lips.

She closed her eyes—but then the kiss was over.

"Ben, I've got to go—I really have to go," she whispered.

"I know," Ben said. "I know."

"Um . . . see you Monday, I guess."

Ben just looked at her—almost as if he didn't believe her. "I hope so, Maddy Mailer. I really hope so."

Seven

O<small>N MONDAY MORNING</small> Malory breezed into homeroom, moving deftly past a swarm of kids blocking the door. Dressed in her faded Gap jeans and a fitted turquoise T-shirt, cropped slightly above the jeans line, Malory felt like less of a total clothing freak—but still intimidated. She noticed that the uniform of choice among Shella and her crew that day consisted of miniskirts, knee-high stockings, cropped tees, and diaphanous blouses. The girls gave her a once-over—not quite as contemptuously as last week, but Malory could tell that her clothes still didn't measure up to their standards. Not that it mattered. She would never dress like them. But still, she felt her face burn under their critical scrutiny.

Ben likes me just the way I am, Malory

consoled herself. She sat down—then she shook her head. *The way I am. . . . Which is what?* Ben liked someone named Maddy Mailer, not Malory Hunter. A girl with black hair, not auburn. For a moment Malory wondered if Ben would like her if he knew who she really was. If he knew how many secrets she had that she could never tell.

She had spent all day Sunday thinking about their afternoon together, reliving their kiss a thousand times. Once her mother had caught her staring off into space, a foolish grin on her face.

"I had no idea tutoring could be such an uplifting experience," Mrs. Hunter had remarked dryly.

Had she suspected anything? Probably not. She'd probably just been thankful that Malory was in a good mood.

Usually Malory moaned and groaned her way through Sunday chores. Part of the reason was because Malory remembered how special Sundays had been when she was a very little girl—dinner with her grandparents and playtime with her cousins afterward. But those memories were so old that they had taken an unreal, dreamlike quality.

The memory of Ben's kiss was burned into her brain with such intensity that she could almost still feel the tingle of his lips on hers.

About a minute before first period was supposed to start, Ben sauntered into class. His eyes immediately went to her desk. He burst into a wide grin. Malory stopped wondering if Ben would like her with auburn hair. Her heart beat loudly as he approached.

He walked right by Shella and the others, without even so much as a look in their direction.

"Hey, Ben!" Shella began. "How was your . . . ?"

"Hi, Maddy," he said.

"Hi," she replied. She cast a glance at Shella, whose eyes had narrowed.

Ben slid into the desk behind her. "I had a great time on Saturday," he said, almost in a whisper.

She turned around, not caring anymore what Shella thought. "Me too," she whispered quickly.

"Want to have lunch together?" he asked.

Malory nodded.

"I'll meet you on the bench outside the cafeteria after fifth period."

"Okay, great," Malory said, her eyes shining.

Ben smiled. "Great."

The bell rang. Malory felt as if she were walking on air as she headed out of the room and up to her first-period English class. It was pretty amazing, she realized. She never felt this way—so happy and free and alive. Well, almost never. But this time there wasn't a piano nearby.

★   ★   ★

Malory paced herself to keep from running through the hallway to meet Ben for lunch. She didn't want to be the first one there—but she didn't want to keep him waiting for too long either.

When Malory got to the bench outside the cafeteria, she looked around. Ben wasn't anywhere in sight. She felt self-conscious. She didn't want to look as if she was waiting for anybody, so she sat down next to the honeysuckle bushes and unwrapped her lunch.

Suddenly she heard a high-pitched giggle. She groaned silently. Shella and Emily and Erin had gathered right behind her, just on the other side of the bushes. Malory nibbled purposefully on her peanut butter and honey sandwich, pretending that eating by herself was the most normal thing in the world. It seemed as if the girls didn't even know she was there.

"So I was, like, 'Dad, you are such a dweeb!'" Erin exclaimed. "Like I'm going to spend your money on *beer?* What a waste! It's for my DKNY sweater!"

"Well, *my* father is worse," started Shella, crunching loudly on something. "He will not increase my clothing allowance at all—not even by, like, twenty dollars! It's so pathetic. And you know what else he said?"

"Get a jo-ob!" they all sang out in unison, then burst into laughter.

89

Malory winced. She felt as if she were listening in on some bad sitcom. She couldn't believe that people really *talked* like this.

"Yeah, like I'm gonna waste my time flipping burgers or asking people their hat size," Shella added. "I think not."

The other girls laughed again.

"Hey, like, where were all the cute guys at your party?" Emily asked, slurping loudly on her drink.

"Very funny," Erin mumbled. "There were lots of cute guys."

"Speaking of cute guys," Emily continued, "what's up with Ben and that dork?"

Malory froze. She felt mildly queasy. As carefully as she could she poked her head around the bushes and snuck a glance—but it was clear they had no idea she was there.

"Oh, Ben is always picking up outcasts," Shella said derisively. "I don't know what it is. He thinks it makes him look, like, more deep as an artist or something."

"I don't kno-ow!" said Erin. "It looks pretty serious to me."

"As if." Shella's voice was firm. "He does this every year. He likes to pretend he's some sort of down-and-out artist. So he picks up some weird loner and pretends he's her boyfriend. It never lasts. Believe me, I've seen it before. But anyway, did you guys check out what Bradley was wearing. . . ."

Malory was no longer listening. Her queasiness had now become gut-wrenching nausea. She couldn't believe that Ben was the type to "pick up some weird loner." Then again, Shella probably considered anyone who didn't wear disgustingly expensive designer clothing or use the word *like* four hundred times per hour to be a "weird loner." Still, it hurt to think of him spending time with another girl. . . .

Where was he anyway?

She looked at her watch. 12:40. He was already ten minutes late.

Was he standing her up?

Just as she was considering taking a walk around the cafeteria to look for him, a shadow fall across her.

She looked up—and nearly shrieked.

She found she was staring into the squinty eyes of a man whose face was pockmarked and pale. He was wearing a heavy black shirt and dark jeans.

Her heart lurched. She was too terrified to speak. She was too terrified to even breathe. Her only thought was: *They've found me. I'm dead.*

"I was wondering if you could do me a favor," the man said in a heavy, raspy voice.

Malory looked around wildly to see if there was any way she could escape. Kids were walking by—but there was no one in her immediate vicinity. Shella and the other girls had departed without her even noticing. If she could knock the guy down and sprint past him, she might be able to make it to school, get her bike, and—

"Can you tell me where a phone is around here?" He smiled slightly. "I got a flat just outside the school, and I really need a tow truck."

Malory's jaw dropped. She felt as if she were going to pass out.

"Hey, are you okay?" the guy asked, looking concerned.

"Yeah, I'm fine," Malory managed in a shaky whisper. *Just totally paranoid.*

He tapped his foot. "So, uh . . ."

"I'm sorry." She shook her head. "I really don't know. But, uh, the office is just through those doors. I'm sure they'll let you use the phone in there."

He smiled. "Thanks, kid."

Malory's body sagged as she watched him disappear into the school building. Her breath was coming in uneven gasps. There had been a perfectly logical explanation. . . .

Wait a minute.

A flat tire? If he had gotten a flat tire, wouldn't he have looked for a pay phone on the street? She glanced around. There must be a hundred kids out here. Why had the man come to *her?*

Suddenly she was no longer relieved. Suddenly she was terrified.

92

Without another moment of hesitation Malory hopped up and began heading toward the cafeteria. She knew she would be much safer inside the school building. They wouldn't try anything in there, would they?

As she drew closer to the doors she became aware of someone yelling: "Maddy! Maddy!"

Maddy? She'd forgotten; that was *her.* She whirled around to see Ben running toward her, waving. "Hey," he said breathlessly. He smiled when he caught up to her.

"Oh, it's you." Malory looked furtively at the cafeteria door.

"I've been calling your name for, like, a minute! Didn't you hear me?"

She swallowed. "No, I'm sorry, I didn't."

Ben frowned. "What's wrong? Is it because I was late? I'm sorry, but it wasn't my fault. Mr. Nordgren had a fit over this sketch I was doing in class. He sent me to the principal's office—"

"No." Malory shook her head. Beads of sweat were forming on her brow. She felt so vulnerable here, so *unprotected.* Somebody could be standing on the roof of a nearby building right now, looking at her through the sights of a rifle. . . .

"Jeez, I'm sorry," he said, grinning. "I'll never be late again! It was unavoidable! Please forgive me!"

Malory was vaguely aware that he was teasing

her, but she was unable to respond. She simply started walking.

"Hey, I was just kidding around," he said, trotting after her. "Come on, Maddy. Don't be mad."

"Look." Malory stopped short and faced him. She was breathing hard. Her face was flushed. "You do not have to be my friend," she blurted. "I'm not even supposed to have friends—" She broke off, shuddering uncontrollably. Why was she doing this to him? It made no sense. His face was ashen, bewildered.

"Ben . . . I'm so sorry . . . you can't . . ." Malory looked into his eyes and did the last thing in the world she wanted to—she burst into tears.

Ben reached out and put his hand on her shoulder. "Please tell me what it is that's going on with you, Maddy," he whispered.

"I can't," she choked. Unable to control herself any longer, she leaned forward and buried her face in his shoulder. He wrapped his arms tightly around her.

"It's okay," he breathed soothingly. "It's okay."

Even as she wept and clung to him, she realized that he probably thought she was crazy. Was he just taking pity on her because he felt sorry for her? Did he really think of her as an outcast, someone to get involved with and later discard? Shella's words drifted through her mind: *It never lasts.* If only Shella knew how true those words really were. But at least—for now, in Ben's arms—she felt safe.

Finally she took a deep breath and stepped away from him.

She noticed that a couple of people were leering at them as they walked by, but Ben didn't seem to care. "Are you all right?" he asked, looking at her closely.

Malory nodded. "Look, I'm sorry about that. I don't know what came over me."

"Don't worry about it," he said.

She knew that she had to give him some sort of explanation—even if it was a lie. She owed him that much. But a plausible excuse wasn't leaping to mind.

"Look, Ben, I'd like to see you later on," she finally said. "We can really talk. I mean it. You know . . . if that's okay with you."

He gave her that lazy grin that had intoxicated her the first moment she ever saw him. "Of course that's okay with me," he said quietly.

"Good." She nodded, collecting herself. The strange man in black who had vanished into the school was now far from her thoughts. If she was with Ben, she would be safe. She was sure of it.

Ben's face brightened. "Hey—I've got a great idea," he said. "Why don't you come to the fireman's fair with me tonight?"

In spite of her flustered state Malory smiled.

"A fireman's fair?" she asked. "I thought those went out in the fifties or something."

He cocked an eyebrow. "Certain parts of L.A. are caught in this weird time warp. Come on. It'll be fun."

A quiet chuckle escaped her lips. One minute this strange girl was crying into his arms, and the next minute he was asking her to a fireman's fair.

"So?" he asked.

"I really shouldn't go out on weeknights," Malory said, avoiding his eyes. She felt as if a tape recorder was running inside her, spewing out a ready-made excuse. The response was automatic. "I have to take care of my brothers after school— and help with dinner. And then do my homework—"

"But you just said you wanted to see me!" he cried.

"I know, I know." She shook her head. "I . . . I'm just crazy, Ben."

"That much is obvious," he said—but his tone was light and forgiving. "Look, I don't take no for an answer, remember? You told me that."

She laughed. "All right. You got yourself a date."

Eight

MALORY TOLD HER parents she was going to the library.

Night had fallen by the time she'd managed to get out of the apartment. When she raced out of the building, she saw that Ben was parked across the street, waiting for her. She knew that she couldn't hide the excitement that sparkled in her eyes. But she didn't care. She *was* excited. For the first time in her life, Malory Hunter was going on a date. The circumstances were less than perfect—she'd had to lie to her parents, after all—but in a way that added to the thrill.

"Folks say it's okay?" he asked as she clambered in.

"More or less." She smiled at him. "I didn't give them the chance to say no."

He grinned mischievously, then put the car in

gear and sped out onto the street. "That's the way to do it, Maddy."

Malory leaned back in the seat and sighed happily.

"I'm glad you're in a better mood," he said.

"Yeah, I guess I was just missing my old home," she said. In a way it was true; she *did* miss her old home—the one in New York. She'd been missing it for eleven years now. And she had been missing it today at school—although, of course, that wasn't why she'd gotten so upset. But admitting to her homesickness certainly wasn't a lie either. She'd made a decision to tell Ben the truth whenever possible, even if the truth was incomplete.

He hesitated. "It must be hard, moving from place to place."

"It is," she admitted quietly. *Please don't ask any more questions about my past,* she silently begged. *Please don't.* Before he had a chance to speak again, she said, "So, does your mom usually let you go out on a school night? That's pretty cool for a teacher. She's really great. Her class is my favorite so far." The words seemed to pour out of her mouth.

Ben shrugged. "When she heard I was taking you, she was totally psyched."

"What do you mean?" Malory asked, her forehead wrinkling.

"She was raving about you tonight at dinner.

We have this friend visiting from New York—he teaches at the Juilliard School. My mother was telling him she's never seen anyone your age with so much talent."

Malory blushed. Mrs. Lerner was bragging about her to someone who taught at Juilliard? It was unbelievable. She didn't even think of her musical ability as talent; it was just a part of her, as natural as breathing or walking. But the words flattered her nonetheless. "Sure, she has," she said, clearing her throat. "She's seen you draw."

Ben laughed as if he didn't believe her. "That's different, Maddy."

She glanced over at him. "How?"

"Well—*anyone* can draw," he said. "I guess I just do it more than most people."

"Come on, Ben." She smiled. "Nobody I know can draw like you. Anyway, it's the same thing for me with the piano. I just do it more than most people."

"Now you're being modest," he said. "My mom told me that you don't even *have* a piano. Face it: You've got a gift."

"Well, so do you," she countered.

Ben flashed her a quick grin. "Okay, I admit it; I'm a genius."

Malory laughed. She had the sudden urge to throw her arms around his neck and kiss him. How could he make her feel like this— so carefree and sure of herself and content all at once, with just a simple, stupid joke?

The Jeep came over the crest of a hill, and Ben pointed out the window. "Hey, check it out."

Malory forced herself to tear her eyes off him. A huge Ferris wheel swam into view, along with the lights of the other rides and games. "Wow," she said. "It really *is* a fair."

"You say that like you've never seen one before. Don't they have fairs where you came from?" he asked teasingly.

Sure, they did—but I wasn't allowed to go, Malory thought. "I guess I just never had the chance to go to one," she said.

His face grew serious. Clearly he hadn't been expecting that kind of sober response. "Well, uh, I'm glad to give you the opportunity," he said uncertainly.

Malory felt bad. She didn't want to say anything that would make him feel awkward or uncomfortable. Maybe lying *was* better—if it would make her seem more normal. She reached over and put her hand on his knee. "I'm glad too," she said.

Malory felt a twinge of nervousness while Ben found a parking place. There were so many strange faces here—so many people who could spot her. And in a crowd like this she could easily get lost or separated from Ben. . . .

They closed the doors and began heading toward the packed fairgrounds. Malory felt Ben squeeze her hand. "What should we do first?" he asked.

"How about the Ferris wheel?" Malory suggested.

Ben grinned. "I was hoping you'd say that."

Suddenly he stopped walking. Malory followed his line of vision. She frowned. Shella and her gang were at the Ferris wheel, arguing over who went in which car.

"Maybe we should try something else first," Ben muttered.

"Good idea," she said

Ben grabbed her arm and began snaking his way through the swarm of people toward a carousel. All at once Malory felt hot and claustrophobic. *Coming here wasn't a good idea,* she thought, glancing out of the corner of her eye at passersby. She kept imagining that people were looking at her. Finally she kept her head down and stared at people's feet pounding across the black asphalt.

"You like merry-go-rounds?" Ben asked.

Malory just nodded. The truth was that merry-go-rounds reminded her of her own life: They were constantly moving, around and around, but they never really went anywhere. She almost laughed. What would Ben think if she said that to him?

"Well, hello there," a deep male voice said beside her.

Malory's head jerked up with a panicked start—only to see Mr. Griffin, her homeroom teacher, standing there with a pretty woman who was holding some cotton candy.

"Hi, Mr. Griffin, Mrs. Griffin," Ben said quickly.

Malory just smiled. She found that her breath was coming in shaky gasps.

"Out on a school night, huh?" Mr. Griffin asked teasingly, raising his eyebrows.

Ben shrugged. "I guess we could say the same for you."

Mr. Griffin laughed. "I guess so. Is your mother here too?"

"Nah." Ben shook his head. "She never goes out on a school night."

"That's a good policy," Mr. Griffin said with a crooked smile. "Well, enjoy yourselves, you two. I'll see you bright and early tomorrow."

Malory stared blankly as Mr. Griffin and his wife disappeared into the crowd.

"It's always fun running into your teachers, huh?" Ben said sarcastically. He looked at her. "Hey—are you okay?" he asked, taking her hand again. "You look like you saw a ghost."

"No, it's just that, uh—" Malory broke off. It was just what? It was just that she thought Mr. Griffin might have been a hit man for the Mob?

"He doesn't care that we're here," Ben said

reassuringly. "My mom's a teacher, remember? I get special privileges."

Malory just smiled. Ben thought she was concerned because a teacher had seen them out on a school night. It was so sweet, so innocent. If only her worries were that trivial.

Ben gazed down at her, his brown eyes twinkling in the spinning lights of the fair. All at once she felt an overwhelming desire to kiss him. Her lips swam forward and met with his, and gradually all the paranoia began to recede. As long as Ben Lerner held her in his arms, she could forget about the misery of her life. As long as she could touch *him,* nothing could touch *her.*

Finally they stepped apart.

Ben took a deep breath. "You're something else, Maddy, you know that?" he murmured huskily.

At the mention of the name "Maddy," Malory almost burst into tears. *I'm something else, all right,* she thought. *Something and someone you can never know.*

Nine

B Y LUNCHTIME THE next day Malory knew she had *definitely* made the wrong decision to go to the fair with Ben. It wasn't that she hadn't had a magical, wonderful, amazingly romantic time—because she had. They'd held hands on the Ferris wheel and kissed while the lights of west L.A. were spread out far below them. She'd even managed to forget about things for a while—until she'd had to go home and tell her parents about the "library."

No: The reason the decision had been such a bad one was because she had slipped from anonymity into a strange kind of instant fame. She began to realize just how popular Ben was. Suddenly several teachers knew her by name. Kids she had never seen before were smiling at her in the halls. Seth and Ben's other good friends started to treat her like she was part of their group. The gossip network among the faculty must have operated no differently than the one among the kids, especially when the well-liked son of a teacher was involved.

It was fun, on the one hand, to be more than a nameless New Girl. On the other hand, it was scary knowing that half the high school could now pick her out in a crowd. Malory was beginning to understand why her parents were so vehement about her learning to act invisible.

But far worse than the greetings and smiles was the feeling she had—the weird, creepy feeling that she was being watched.

She'd had it before, many times. But for some reason this time it was more pronounced. She felt like she was being watched with binoculars; as if every nuance of her face was being studied and judged. Four hours had passed, and she still hadn't caught a glimpse of anyone suspicious— but she was positive someone was there.

As she sat down at her usual spot outside the cafeteria, Malory scanned the lunchroom crowd. Maybe that guy with the flat tire from yesterday had altered his appearance somehow and was posing as a teacher. . . .

"Hey!"

Malory jumped.

Ben sat down beside her. "Earth to Maddy. Are you with us? We're losing contact." He dug his hand into a brown paper bag and pulled out a bag of pretzels.

Malory forced a smile. "How's it going?" She was vaguely aware that Ben had been standing there and talking to her for a minute or so, but she hadn't heard any of it.

"Hmmm." He eyed her suspiciously. "Did you hear a word of what I just said?"

Malory blushed.

"Well, it's nice to know you're so captivated by my conversation," he said, grinning wryly. "Anyway, as I was saying, on Saturday there's someplace I really want to take you. It's kind of out of the way, but it's, like, my favorite place. Would you be into that?" He looked at her expectantly.

"Of course," she said. She hoped her answer sounded enthusiastic. She didn't want him to notice how distracted she was. He might ask her what was wrong—yet again. She struggled to keep her eyes on his handsome face, but they longed to dart around as if they had a will of their own.

Ben laughed. "Wouldn't you at least like to know where it is?"

"What? Of course I would. Sure." Malory heard herself say the words, but her mind was drifting further and further away. Where would someone position himself if he wanted to watch her? The roof? No—she had already looked a dozen times. The basketball court? Ridiculous. Then a patch of black caught her eye. *There!* Through the window, in the back of the cafeteria, was a man she had never seen before. He was dressed in a dark suit.

In an instant Malory was on her feet.

". . . and then we'll—" Ben broke off. "Maddy?"

Malory glanced down at his bewildered face, but her gaze was drawn back to the stranger as if with a magnet. He was sitting at a table with some students, chatting amiably.

Then he looked up and caught her eye.

She desperately wanted to look away, but she was mesmerized—frozen in horror like a wild animal caught in the headlights of a speeding car. In that instant the man gave her a slow, lazy smile and got up from the table. His eyes never left her face.

"I have to go," she gasped—and she began walking away rapidly. *I can't endanger Ben,* she thought. *If that guy sees me talking to him, he might think that Ben somehow knows.* At that moment her only desire was to put as much distance in between herself and Ben as possible.

"Wait!" Ben called after her. "What do you mean? I thought you wanted to hear about Saturday. Where are you going?"

"I . . . I just remembered something I have to do. It's very important—I'm sorry! I'll see you after school!" She broke into a run.

Breathing hard, Malory dashed through the double doors of the school and up the stairs to room 2007, where her fifth-period social studies class met. The classroom was empty, so she ducked inside. She sat in the back, facing the door. It would be at least another fifteen minutes before it filled up, but at least she was safe for now. She was pretty sure the man would look outside for her first.

All at once a peculiar calm settled over her. It was strange: Whenever she was in any kind of real danger, she was able to relax. It was only when her imagination got the best of her that she started to panic. But now she was certain that she was in dire trouble. The Mafia was here. The man had seen her. He had smiled. And now he was coming to look for her.

How did they find us? she wondered. *Was there a leak in the FBI?*

There must have been. After the experience in Lincoln Hills she was starting to think that the FBI and the Mafia weren't necessarily separate organizations. No one from the Mafia could have found them way out there. *Unless* someone on the inside had told them.

She hopped out of her seat and walked to the window. Kids were already starting to head back into the school building for the start of next period. There was no sign of the man in the dark suit. She began pacing around agitatedly. For a brief moment her thoughts wandered to Ben. He was probably sitting there wondering why he had decided to get involved with a schizophrenic.

How could she let him know she wasn't crazy?

She couldn't, she realized. And besides, she probably *was* crazy.

The day dragged endlessly until Mrs. Lerner's music appreciation class. At least Malory hadn't seen the man in the suit again. But she had been totally incapable of concentrating on her school-work. On several occasions teachers had scolded her for not listening. A few of them even mentioned "being out on a school night"—much to the delight of the other students. Malory couldn't believe it. How did everyone find out about her date so fast? Why was it that human beings couldn't just keep their mouths shut? She'd spent her whole life keeping her mouth shut. Some of these people could learn a thing or two from her. But people liked to gossip.

Maybe this time someone's idle gossip had reached the wrong ears . . . the wrong person had heard something about the Hunter family and that's why she was being stalked. It all came down to people telling other people secrets.

As she turned into the corridor that led to the music room, she froze. Mrs. Lerner was talking to the man in the dark suit. They were laughing and talking together as if they were old friends who had just accidentally run into each other. Then Mrs. Lerner shook his hand warmly.

Malory was suddenly angry. Couldn't Mrs. Lerner see through his facade? The guy was most likely a cold-blooded killer—and he was using Mrs. Lerner to get to Malory. But there was no point waiting around to ponder the situation. She had to leave—now. She turned and tore down the hall just as Mrs. Lerner caught a glimpse of her standing there.

"Malory, wait, I want to talk to you!" Mrs. Lerner called after her. "There's somebody here who . . ."

But she didn't stop. She glanced over her shoulder—but luckily the man wasn't running after her. She took the back stairs that led to the basement exit, then dashed out of the building to where her bike was kept. Her mind was racing. She would meet the boys first—before going home and making any calls. If she pedaled fast, she might be able to beat the man to the twins' elementary school. *If* he was alone.

Then she paused.

Why was she running? The man would just follow her. The safest thing for her to do would be to stay in Mrs. Lerner's classroom. Yes, she would just walk calmly back to the classroom and sit there—and stay there until the man went away.

But as she was coming back up the stairs, she saw something that made her heart stop.

There, right at the top of the steps, was Ben. And he was talking to the man in the suit.

She froze in the middle of the stairwell. She was paralyzed with fear. How could she have gotten innocent people like Ben and Mrs. Lerner involved? How did they even know to approach the Lerners in the first place? Then she had a horrible thought: They must have seen her going to the Lerners' house to play piano. They knew where the Lerners lived.

Ben noticed her standing there. At first he smiled at her, but his smile faded when he saw the expression on her face. "Maddy, come here," he called. "I want you to meet someone."

Malory didn't know what to do. She didn't have time to think. So she turned around and started to bolt down the stairs. She heard Ben calling after her, but she kept running, navigating herself down the stairs and then through the crowded hallway. She could feel people watching her, but she didn't care. She just wanted to get away. As she was almost at the end of the hall, she tripped on a backpack and fell to the ground.

Ben had been right behind her. Now he knelt down to her on the floor with a bewildered look on his face. "Maddy," he panted, out of breath, "what's going on? I was about to introduce you to my mom's friend, John Slattery."

Malory's eyes widened. She felt herself trembling.

"Mr. Slattery is also an admissions officer at the Juilliard School in New York. He's the one I was telling you about." Ben grabbed Malory's hand. "What were you running from?"

Malory saw Mr. Slattery walking down the hall toward them with a stunned expression on his face. She looked back at Ben. *His mother's friend from Juilliard?* She felt a sickening wave of nausea wash through her entire body. For an instant everything around her seemed to look strange and wavy. There was a rushing noise in her ears. Then it all seemed to disappear in a funnel of darkness. She felt herself falling, and her vision went black. . . .

"Maddy? Maddy—are you all right?"

Malory blinked several times. She found herself staring up at Ben's face. But it seemed odd, somehow. It was floating sideways in midair. She blinked again and realized that her head was on something soft.

"Are you all right?" he repeated.

Suddenly she became aware that she was lying on Ben's lap. Or more specifically, she was lying by the lockers in the hallway, and her head was in Ben's lap. She sat up abruptly and saw that a small crowd had gathered around them. Mr. Slattery from the Juilliard School was nowhere in sight.

"Oh, no," Malory moaned.

"What's wrong?" Ben asked anxiously. "Are you hurt?"

"No, no—I'm fine," she mumbled. The group of students huddled around them began to disperse. "I can't believe I did that." Her voice rose. "I'm such an idiot!"

Ben just stared at her.

Malory didn't know whether to laugh hysterically or to burst into tears. A man from the Juilliard School had come here to meet her—and she had run away from him like a maniac, then passed out. Great. He was probably dying to have her enroll as a student now. She shook her head. "Where did, uh . . . ?"

"Mr. Slattery go?" Ben finished gently. "Well, after your psychotic episode, I think he realized that you didn't want to see him."

Malory managed a halfhearted grin.

"Actually I think he just went to alert my mother that you aren't going to be in class today," Ben added, brushing a lone strand of dyed black hair out of her face.

Malory put her head in her hands. She'd just had the opportunity to meet someone who worked at the place where she'd dreamed of going her whole life—and she'd blown it. She started to get angry again, but the anger quickly died. What did it matter anyway? Even if she hadn't just made a total fool of herself, she had no hope of going there in the first place. Juilliard was a nice dream—and it was totally out of the question. She couldn't go back to New York and live there. It was definitely not safe in New York.

Ben smiled sympathetically.

"Well, I . . . uh, I guess I ought to go home and lie down," Malory said, standing up and brushing off her clothes.

"What happened?" Ben asked.

She shrugged. "I fainted."

"I *know* that, Maddy. I mean, why were you running from Mr. Slattery?"

"Oh . . ." Malory averted her eyes. She tried to think of an excuse, but her mind was still fuzzy and unclear. "I, uh . . . I thought he was someone else."

Ben laughed. "Yeah, I could see that. Maybe . . . a serial killer you knew in a former life?"

"Something like that." Malory said. She shifted on her feet, still too embarrassed to meet Ben's eyes.

Ben opened his mouth as if he were going to ask her something else, then closed it. "Come on, Maddy, let me take you home."

She looked at him. "But what about class? Don't you have something this period?"

"My mom's a teacher, remember?" He winked. "I'm untouchable. If I miss anything, my mom will just get me the answers to the next quiz."

Malory smiled in spite of herself. She suddenly realized that she owed him some kind of explanation. He deserved *some* excuse at the very least, considering how rude she had been to this friend of his family's. Ben and his mother had tried to do her a favor, and she had simply freaked out. And now Ben was skipping class to take her home. She felt ill.

But what could she possibly say? She was just going to have to lie again.

"You sure you don't want to try to meet Mr. Slattery again real quick before we go?" Ben suggested quietly.

Malory shook her head. "Forget it. I mean, I really appreciate everything you did, but it's way too embarrassing." She started walking down the steps.

"But what about Juilliard?"

What about it? she thought dismally.

"Come on, you have to tell me what went on just now." Ben caught up to her and searched her face as they walked down the hall. "Please, Maddy. You can trust me, you know."

Malory looked helplessly into his eyes. *I know I can trust you. I just don't want to put you in danger.* It was so hard to lie to him. Finally, when they reached the stairs, she stopped.

"This is the best I can give you," she started, praying she could tell him at least some semblance of the truth.

"There happens to be a certain group of people

that my family and I don't particularly like," she said awkwardly. "I've known them for a long time—almost my whole life. They scare me, and . . . uh, I disapprove of the way they do things."

Ben frowned. "You mean, like a political group or something?"

"Well, sort of. More like a secret club. Anyway, whenever I see someone from this group or even just *think* I see someone," she mumbled, "I kind of freak out."

"And I suppose you thought Mr. Slattery was one of this group?"

Malory nodded hopefully.

But Ben just laughed. "That's it? You expect me to buy that? That is so lame!"

Malory cringed. He was right. He probably thought she was joking. "I know it sounds totally ridiculous, but that's the truth, and it's the best I can do right now."

Ben sighed. "So it's the Hare Krishnas that make you feel like this," he muttered.

Malory leaned close to him. Poor Ben. Why was he even wasting his time with her? He should just go find someone normal, someone who could offer him the honesty he deserved.

The next thing she knew, she was hugging him. Touching him wasn't much of a response to his question—but at least it made her feel as if she could make it through the rest of the day without having a complete breakdown.

Ten

AFTER THAT INCIDENT the week passed fairly quickly. Malory no longer felt as though someone were watching her around every corner. And although she had to be home each night to help out with dinner and the twins, she was able to meet Ben after school every day. Thankfully he didn't ask any more questions. They would just hang out and talk about music, or art, or all the things Shella and her friends were probably doing—anything that would make the two of them laugh.

By Saturday—yes, she couldn't believe it—she actually felt semidecent.

The morning was gray and overcast with a steady, constant drizzle. Malory watched the gray clouds out the window as she ironed her turquoise T-shirt.

117

"I thought it never rains in California," Tommy muttered grumpily as he and Mike watched cartoons on the couch.

"It only rains when you really want to go outside," Malory joked with him, turning off the iron and unplugging it. She was determined that nothing, not even the lousy weather, was going to spoil her day.

"I hate to ask you this, Mal, but do you think you could stick close to the house today?" her mother asked casually as she set the kitchen table for breakfast. "If the boys are going to spend a lot of time inside, I'm going to need some help around here."

Malory froze. She was meeting Ben at ten. *There is no way I am canceling this day.* She took a deep breath.

"I'm sorry, Mom," she answered quietly. "I have plans today."

"Really?" Her mother looked mildly surprised. "What are you doing?"

"Well, I'm going to Mrs. Lerner's at ten." Malory had her lie all ready. "She said I could play the piano there all day if I wanted to. Then I was going to go to the library and study."

"Well, why don't you study at home?" her mother suggested.

"Because I'm doing a paper and I need to use some of the reference books at the library. Besides, Mom," Malory added truthfully, "it's kind of crowded in here. It's a little hard to concentrate."

Malory already had a fake topic planned out for her paper—a ten-pager on Mozart for history. She knew her mother would buy that. But her mom just smiled and said, "Okay, honey. I understand."

"Thanks." Malory tried not to sound too relieved. She knew that her mother was more worried than usual; she was always more jittery on the weekends, when her time was less structured. But nothing was going to stop Malory from spending this day with Ben.

Almost to make up for her deception, Malory started cleaning furiously. She polished the little table in the living room, which Tommy and Mike were always leaving sticky and disgusting. She would clean for another ten minutes—then she would take off and meet Ben at their appointed meeting place.

Just then the intercom buzzer from downstairs rang.

Malory stopped scrubbing. She looked at her mother apprehensively.

Who could be buzzing them? No one was supposed to know their address—no one but a few select people in the FBI. They kept only a post office box number so they could receive school mail.

Cautiously Mrs. Hunter depressed the

speak button and asked, "Who's there?"

Through the static-filled connection a familiar voice crackled into the room. "Ben Lerner. I'm a friend of Maddy's."

Malory's brief panic was replaced with a different kind of fear—the fear of being found out by her mother. She instantly lunged for the speak button. "I'll be right down," she shouted into the intercom.

Her mother looked at her in confusion. "Malory, I didn't know you were expecting a friend—"

"Oh, it's just Mrs. Lerner's son—he's in my homeroom. I forgot; he offered to pick me up," Malory interrupted, making it up as she went along. Why had he decided to come here? How had he even figured out which apartment was hers? But she couldn't worry about those things now. "He was coming from an early appointment and he was on the way," she finished.

Mrs. Hunter chewed her lip. "Well, that's nice," she said uncertainly. "But you know that we're not supposed to let anyone know where we live—"

"Don't worry," Malory stated forcefully, intending to end the discussion right there.

"Malory's got a boyfriend! Malory's got a boyfriend!" the twins chanted in chorus.

"Shut up!" Malory said, blushing furiously.

She slipped on a blue windbreaker for the rain and dashed toward the door.

"I think it might be a good idea to introduce me to your friend. Why not invite him up?" Mrs. Hunter asked, examining Malory's reddening face closely.

"Mom, he's not a friend—he's just Mrs. Lerner's son. Gotta go." Malory flung herself out into the hall before her mother could ask any more questions.

"When will you be home?" Mrs. Hunter called.

"I'll call you!"

Feeling light and free, she flew down the stairs to where Ben was waiting, just outside the entrance of the apartment complex. She burst out the door and stopped just short of throwing herself into his arms. "Hi!" she cried, her dark blue eyes sparkling.

"Hi, yourself," Ben said.

Suddenly Ben's lips were touching hers— gently at first, then with greater intensity. Their bodies melded together as they kissed, clinging to each other as if no one else in the world existed.

Coming to her senses, Malory pulled away and glanced around them. Ben didn't seem to notice.

"Boy, am I glad to see you," he whispered.

"Me too," Malory whispered back—still

reeling in shock from the passion of Ben's kiss. "But wait—what are you doing here?"

He grinned. "Why? You're not happy to see me?"

"No." She shook her head, flustered. "It's just . . . why did you pick me up here? How did you find my address? I mean, my parents would freak—"

"Look, Maddy, it wasn't hard to guess which apartment is yours. It was the only buzzer that was unmarked; you don't have a label yet," he interrupted dryly. "And I picked you up here because . . . I was hoping that you might break down and introduce me to your parents. I figured since you met my mom, I might be able to meet yours."

"But—but . . . your mom is my teacher," Malory mumbled. "Of course I would meet her."

Ben paused. For a brief moment he almost looked angry. Then he said, "Of course you would." He turned and began walking through the rain toward the Jeep.

Malory didn't know what to say. She wanted to be mad at him. After all, he had found out where she lived without her permission. But it wasn't his fault. Nothing was his fault. At that moment she wanted to run back upstairs and shout to her mother—and the world—that she was in love with Ben Lerner.

Yes—she realized that now. That's precisely what she felt. She was in love. For the first time in her life, Malory Hunter was in love.

Ben stopped when he reached the car. "You coming?" he called.

She dashed across the street and hopped in.

Eleven

"SO YOU HAVEN'T told me where we're going," Malory said after they'd been driving for about half an hour. She had been staring at the beach off the freeway and flipping idly through the stations on the radio.

"You'll see," Ben said with a secret smile. "The weatherman said the sky was going to clear, and I think he might have gotten it right."

Malory squinted up at the sky. It was still raining, but Ben was right: It looked as if the sun was poised to break through the blanket of clouds at any second.

"You know, I'm sorry I didn't call you first— before I came over," Ben said, keeping his eyes firmly planted on the road. "But I don't have your phone number. You're not listed, you know."

Malory forced her face to remain blank. "It takes a while to get listed."

"Uh-huh. I even tried to get your number from the school—but they wouldn't give it out, not even when I pinched my nose and pretended to be a sweepstakes announcer who'd pulled your name out of a prize bin."

"Imagine that," Malory said, allowing herself a smile. Actually she was relieved to know that the school wouldn't give out her phone number. It was nice to know they respected the Hunters' privacy.

"Yeah, they said somebody had just tried a trick like that," Ben said ruefully. "Just the other day, as a matter of fact. Mrs. Craft in the office told me, 'Sorry, pal—it didn't work then, and it's not gonna work this time either.'"

"What did they mean, 'tried a trick like that'?" Malory asked, immediately suspicious.

Ben shrugged. "Guess maybe other people have tried to get somebody's number that way before. Anyway, they pegged me as a phony and wouldn't say a thing."

Malory's breath was coming faster. "Did somebody call and asked for my number, specifically my number, before you did?" she pressed him, her voice rising slightly.

"I don't know, Maddy. They didn't say." He glanced at her. "Is it important? Does it have anything to do with this 'group' you were telling me about?"

Malory hesitated. Was that sarcasm in his voice? No, the harshness was closer to anger—anger at her for not telling him the truth. She wished she could tell him that it *did* have something to do with the group, but not in any way she could explain. She only thought of that guy with the flat tire, the guy who had been looking for a phone. "No," she said finally. "It isn't important."

She stared out the window, past Ben's head, at the vast expanse of ocean. The constant surf pounding against the shore was mesmerizing.

You're just being paranoid again, she scolded herself. *Shake it off and forget it. Nobody's called the school looking for you, and that's that.*

All at once the sun broke through the clouds, dazzling in its sudden brightness. Malory quickly shifted in her seat and looked behind her, then saw what she was looking for: the broad arc of a rainbow.

"Oh, look, Ben—a rainbow," Malory exclaimed. "Quick, close your eyes and make a wish."

"Uh . . . I don't think I'll close my eyes, if that's okay with you," Ben said. "It's probably not the best idea when I'm behind the wheel. Does it work if you wish with your eyes open?"

Malory didn't answer. Her eyes were already closed, and she was wishing the same wish she always did: *Please let us be a normal family. Please keep us safe from those men.* Only this time she added one more part: *Please let L.A. be the last place we ever live.*

Then Malory opened her eyes. She looked over at Ben, who'd been watching her while she wished. She smiled, a little embarrassed.

"I never heard of wishing on a rainbow," he said. "Wishing on a star, maybe, but not a rainbow."

"Oh, it's just something my parents started when I was a kid. I was five, and my brothers were just babies. We were driving in the car, and it had been pouring all night, and I was crying. The sun started to rise, and there was this incredible rainbow. So I guess to stop me from crying, my dad pointed out the rainbow and told me to make a wish. I remember it really clearly. It was the first time we . . ." Malory stopped, realizing she'd gotten carried away with the memory.

"The first time you what?" Ben prodded.

"The first time we moved," Malory improvised.

"Really? Where did you move from?"

"Oh, I don't remember anymore," Malory answered vaguely.

"You don't remember where you're from," Ben said dryly. His tone was accusatory. "I thought you said you missed your old home!"

"I told you before, I'm from a lot of places—I don't remember all of them," Malory whispered tremulously. "I meant that I missed—"

"Look, Maddy," Ben interrupted, softening his tone. "I'm sorry. I don't really care where you're from. All I care about is that you're here now—and with me."

Malory just nodded. She wanted to tell him that she felt the same way—but it would be far easier to keep her mouth closed.

After driving several more minutes Ben took an exit off the highway, then turned sharply up a canyon road. On one side Malory could see the breathtaking green-and-brown-spotted edges of the canyon as it sliced through the mountains and, on the other side, the Pacific Ocean, which sparkled like a sea of diamonds and seemed to go on forever. Overhead loomed a huge expanse of sky, mostly inhabited by thick white and gray clouds but with rays of sun peeping out every now and then. Malory rolled down her window. The air was cool and clean and sweet. She inhaled deeply and smiled with complete satisfaction.

Ben pulled off the road into a little parking area by the head of a trail. "We're here," he announced, cutting the engine.

For a while they just sat in the car, without saying a word. That was one of the things Malory loved about Ben: He didn't feel the need to talk all the time. He knew there was a time and place for talk, and a time and place for silence.

Malory smiled. For some reason, at this very moment she was feeling the most relaxed she had felt in weeks. "It's like we're the only two people in the world," she said quietly, leaning back in her seat and turning her face to the warm sun.

"That's exactly how I feel," Ben said.

"What do you do when you come up here?"

"Mostly sketch."

She felt him take her hand and start to play with her slender fingers. His fingertips seemed soft, almost permeable. She squeezed each one, luxuriating in the sensation.

"Did you ever—oh, never mind." Malory stopped herself. She was about to ask him if he ever brought anyone else up here, but why spoil the moment? She couldn't make any long-term commitments, so she had absolutely no right to feel jealous.

"What?" he asked.

"Nothing." She smiled. "It was silly."

"Okay, but you can ask me anything you want, you know."

"I know," Malory said quietly. But how could she ask him something personal when he couldn't do the same for her?

Gently he folded her into his arms, pressing her into his chest, resting his chin on her soft dark hair. He held her close, and they basked in the light breeze that swept through the Jeep. Malory closed her eyes. For a split second she felt just the way she did when she was playing her piano. Like she was floating above the world, higher and higher out of harm's way. It was a happiness she'd never expected to feel with another person. She shivered involuntarily.

"Are you cold?" Ben asked.

"No—just happy," she said. She sighed and leaned apart from him. "I was just thinking . . . you know, the only times I ever feel this great are when I'm playing the piano." She smiled sadly. "Sounds pathetic, doesn't it?"

"Not in the least," he said seriously. "The only times I ever feel really happy are when I draw." He laughed once. "You know, you can still meet Mr. Slattery if you want to sometime. Maybe next time he comes out west."

Malory just shrugged. "I don't know. . . ." All at once she was seized with a strange, wistful sorrow. She could never keep a lid on her emotions when she was around him; one second she wanted to scream with joy—and the next she wanted to sob uncontrollably. *This is never going to work. He can't get involved in any part of my life. He can't even ask me anything.*

"You don't have to, though," Ben said quickly.

"No, it's just, um . . . I think I need some more piano lessons before I think about anything like a conservatory. Especially one like Juilliard."

"Oh, yeah?" Ben raised his eyebrows. "My mom doesn't think so. And she's a pro."

Malory smiled at him. "Yeah, but *my* mom does. That's what she talks about sometimes. She says someday I'll have piano lessons, and someday . . ." Her voice faded. *And someday I'll have friends. And someday I'll have a boyfriend. . . .*

"Do you remember what you said to me on Monday?" he asked quietly. "You know, when you thought I blew you off at lunch?"

Malory hesitated. She must have said something to make him suspicious. "No, what did I say?"

"You said, 'I'm not supposed to have friends.'" He looked at her closely. "What did that mean?"

"It meant . . . it just meant . . . ," Malory stammered, but she couldn't think of an excuse. "I don't really want to talk about my family," she said lamely, looking down so she wouldn't have to meet Ben's inquiring gaze.

"I know. You never want to talk about your family. But I want to *know* about you. I want to know about your family—where you're from, what you did before. I want to meet your parents and your brothers." He squeezed her hands tightly. "It's important, Maddy."

Maddy, she said to herself, disgusted and ashamed. *You wouldn't think it was so important if you knew that Maddy isn't even my real name.*

131

"You will, sometime," she breathed in a shaky voice. "Really."

"That's a lie—and we both know it," he said gravely. "But I just want to understand why. I want to know why you're never going to tell me anything about yourself. Why don't you want me to know you?"

"I . . . it's not that—" Malory faltered.

"Can't you see that it's important?" Ben took Malory by the shoulders, trying to make her meet his gaze.

Malory shivered. She took a deep breath, then looked into his brown eyes.

"Okay, Ben," she said, searching his face. "I'm going to tell you something. And I don't want you to hate me, okay?"

His eyes flickered. "I promise. I could never hate you."

"Well . . . it's true that I can't talk about my family or where we used to live or anything like that. But I'd like to. I'd love to tell you all about us and where we used to live, and everything that makes me who I am." She paused. "But there's a problem. And the worst part of the problem is that I can't tell you what the problem is. . . ." Suddenly her voice broke, and tears welled up in her eyes.

"It's okay," Ben soothed, hugging her close again. "It's okay."

"No, it's not," she wept. "Because I'm *never*

132

going to tell you anything about my family. I'm never going to tell you anything about my past, where I used to live, things I used to do. I'm never going to tell you. It's going to be a secret forever. Do you understand that?"

"You know, Maddy," Ben said quietly, "if you've done something or been involved in something that you're afraid to tell me about—you don't have to be." He lifted her face and wiped away her tears.

She smiled weakly. "I know. But—"

"First of all I would never, *ever* tell another soul anything that you told me in secret." He took her head in both hands. "Second, nothing you could have done—nothing you could ever do—would change the way I feel about you."

In that instant Malory knew she had never been so close to telling anyone the truth. She bit the inside of her cheek. She longed to just open up and tell him everything: how they'd been running for so long, how much danger they were in, how she'd never had a close friend in all these years, how music was her only solace. But looking into his serious, sincere face, Malory realized that it was impossible. She had already endangered him enough by telling him what she had.

"I only want to talk about *now*. Us. Just you and me," she said fiercely. "Because now is all I have. Now is the only thing I'm sure about."

"But don't you trust me—" he protested.

"I do, I do." Malory quieted him by putting her fingers gently over his lips. "But it doesn't make any difference. Ben, if you care about me at all—if you care about *us,* then please . . . don't ask any more questions. Can you do that?"

"Okay, Maddy," Ben said softly, taking her in his arms and stroking her hair. "I can do that for you."

Twelve

IT WAS SEVEN o'clock by the time the black Jeep rolled up in front of Malory's apartment complex. The wet streets glistened in the waning light.

"Can I see you tomorrow?" Ben asked, turning off the car.

Malory thought a moment. What could she tell her mother? Extra tutoring lessons? After today her mother probably wouldn't buy it.

Ben waited patiently, but his eyes portrayed his eagerness.

Malory reached over and gently put her hand on Ben's knee. "Call me tomorrow morning, okay? I'll know then."

"Okay," Ben said, somewhat reluctantly. Suddenly his eyes brightened. "Wait. I want to show you something." He reached over the back of the driver's seat and grabbed a backpack.

"What is it?" Malory asked.

"Just some drawings," he said, rummaging through the sack and pulling out a small sketchbook. He flipped through a couple of pages and handed it to her.

Malory's eyes widened. The book was open to an unfinished pencil sketch of a seascape. She instantly recognized it as the view from the canyon trail along which they had walked today.

"Wow," she murmured. She began flipping through the pages. The book was filled with dozens of unfinished landscapes, obviously done at different times of the day, with different light and at different angles. There were pages and pages of mountains and the ocean that were drawn from the same spot but were all somehow subtly different: a shadow here, a bush there, a figure on the beach. She was awed at how beautifully detailed Ben's drawings were—down to the smallest flower and scraggliest ball of brush.

"These are amazing, Ben," Malory said. "You're an amazing artist."

"Thanks," Ben said simply.

"How come you don't finish most of them?"

Ben shrugged. "I guess because I'm never at the canyon long enough, and when I go back, the light's always different or something else is. Sometimes I wish I could just run away and live up there."

"I know what you mean. I know all about wanting to run away," Malory said absently.

Ben glanced over at her. "You do? You've thought about running away?" His voice was insistent.

Malory laughed nervously. "Oh, you know, the usual," she replied. She handed his sketchbook back to him. "Don't all teenagers want to run away?"

"Yeah, Maddy—and you're just like every other teenager." He sighed and stuffed the sketchbook back into his bag.

Malory opened her mouth, but no words would come. *I don't want to spoil this day,* she thought. *I won't let it happen.*

"You better get going," Ben said quietly. He tossed his backpack in the backseat, then started the engine again. "You don't want your mother to think you've been kidnapped or anything."

She probably already has, Malory thought miserably. She tried to smile.

"Maddy . . . um, if you don't mind—would it be all right if I got your number?"

"Of course it would," she found herself saying. A little voice in her head was sounding an alarm, but she ignored it. She trusted Ben. Giving him her phone number wouldn't put her in any danger. She had to demonstrate that she cared about him enough to give him *something.*

After she said the seven digits, Ben repeated

them to himself several times, then smiled happily. "Thanks," he said.

"Thank you," Malory whispered. "I had a great time today."

"So did I." He leaned forward and kissed her lightly on the lips.

Malory felt blood rushing to her cheeks. "I better go," she said quickly. She fumbled for the door handle and hopped out of the Jeep.

"I'll call you!" Ben yelled as he roared away.

What have I done? she wondered, staring at his car disappearing down the road.

Her stomach dropped. Revealing her phone number was so stupid. Her parents had specifically told her not to give their phone number out to anyone. If Ben called the house, her parents would be furious. And what if someone were watching them? What if someone knew where to find Ben?

She couldn't afford to think those thoughts. Worry would drive her to insanity.

As Malory turned and slowly walked toward the apartment complex she noticed a black sedan parked a little ways down the block. It was the only car on the street. She glanced at it surreptitiously. Did it look familiar? Had she seen it before? She dredged her memory, trying to remember all the cars she'd seen park in the area—but it was impossible.

Maybe she should take a closer look.

Without being obvious, Malory changed direction and decided to stroll by and check out the plates. California. That was a good sign. Holding her breath, she inched closer to the sedan.

Just then a young woman, somewhere around thirty, stepped out of the car, dressed in a sweat suit. Malory stared at her. She definitely did *not* look like Mafia material. She looked like a . . . well, like a yuppie. Breathing a loud, heavy sigh of relief, Malory turned quickly on her heel and headed for the door.

The lingering fragrance of tomato sauce floated by her as she bounded up the stairs to her apartment. She threw open the door and called, "I'm home!"—then glanced in the kitchen. A pot of water was boiling. The sauce was sitting on the stove, simmering. Spaghetti, uncooked, rested alongside the stove top. Malory felt a pang of guilt. They were obviously waiting for her.

"I'm home," Malory called again tentatively, entering the darkened living room. The flickering light of the television revealed the unconcerned faces of Mike and Tommy.

"Hey, Mal," the boys said in unison, barely turning their heads.

"Where's Mom?" Malory asked, looking around the small apartment.

"She's in her room," Mike began.

"Yeah—she had a bad headache. So she had to lie down for a second," Tommy finished.

Malory frowned. That was odd; there was water boiling on the stove, but her mother had decided to lie down? It didn't make any sense. *Something must be wrong.* "Where's Dad?" she asked.

"Work," Tommy replied.

Malory sighed. At least the boys didn't sense that anything was awry. She tiptoed down the hall and into her parents' bedroom. It wasn't much: a king-size mattress resting in the middle of the room on the floor, flanked by a small digital alarm clock and a small table lamp. A box of tissues lay on the floor right by the foot of the mattress. Mrs. Hunter was stretched out on her back with her eyes closed.

At the sound of Malory's entrance her eyelids fluttered open.

"Malory," she said, a look of relief washing over her face.

Malory felt awful. No wonder she'd come in here—she was probably worried sick about her daughter. "Mom, I'm really sorry I'm so late and I didn't call . . . ," she began all in a rush.

"It's okay, Mal. It's okay," Mrs. Hunter said. "I knew you would be home soon. I knew you would." Her voice seemed strained—as if she were holding something back.

"What's wrong?" Malory asked.

Mrs. Hunter's brow furrowed. "I got a phone call," she began slowly. "Your grandmother passed away." She paused again, her voice quavering. "Last week. And . . . I only found out today." She covered her face with her hands and began shaking with silent sobs.

"Oh, Mom . . ." Malory felt sick. She moved swiftly beside the bed and threw her arms around her mother's shaking shoulders. "I'm sorry. I'm so sorry," she whispered. Her grief was compounded with anger. What was the use of looking forward to a normal life again if there was no one left to go back to?

But Malory felt something else as well. She felt scared.

In all the years of picking up and leaving—driving hours upon hours into the night and starting all over again—Malory had never seen her mother break down. She'd always been calm and cool. But something like this . . . something like this was bound to take its toll.

"How did it happen?" Malory asked.

With a deep sigh, Mrs. Hunter pulled herself together and began speaking. "Heart failure. It happened about a week ago. Dad tried to reach me. . . ." The tears started filling her eyes again.

Malory reached behind her and grabbed a tissue, then handed it to her.

"Thank you, honey," she said with a sniff. "My father tried to reach me—he called the agency. They said it was too soon to contact me. He begged—my mother was asking for me,

Mal—but the damned FBI wouldn't give him our damned number." She dabbed her eyes, then hurled the wad of tissue away from her. "They wouldn't even let me have a final word with my own mother!" Suddenly she was crying again. She buried her face in her hands.

Malory was too shocked to speak—too shocked by the news, too torn by her mother's pain. She couldn't deal with this on her own. She thought of her grandmother, whose face she could barely remember, hooked up to tubes and machines, trying to get someone to contact her daughter so she could see her one last time before she died. Tears came to Malory's eyes as well.

What was the point of it all, she thought. What was the point of always being on the run, always looking over your shoulder, never having anyone outside the family to confide in? If you couldn't see your dying mother, or talk to your sisters, or have a boyfriend . . . what was the point?

Malory pulled away from her. "Let's call Dad, okay?"

Mrs. Hunter raised her head. Her tear-filled eyes looked into Malory's face. "Oh, Mal," she said, drawing a shuddering breath. "I don't want to bother him. He's got so much on his mind."

"You know—this is crazy," Malory said quietly.

"What did you say?"

"It's insane, Mom," Malory said angrily. "Here we are, pretending to be like a normal family; I'm playing the piano in the high-school orchestra, Daddy's out at his job, you're making dinner like Mrs. Brady, and it's all a lie! You're calling Dad—and he's coming home now!"

"Malory, this is no time for hysterics," Mrs. Hunter said, struggling to regain her composure.

"That's not true. It's a very good time for hysterics. For God's sake, Mom, your mother just died—and you don't want to call Dad because he has too much on his mind! What about *you!*" Her voice rose to a shout. "You can't even go to the funeral!"

Her mother's face took on a pale, horrified expression. Malory realized she was staring over her shoulder at the door. She whirled around.

Mike and Tommy were standing side by side in the doorway, wide-eyed and fearful. "What's wrong, Mom?" Tommy asked.

Briskly Mrs. Hunter rose from her bed. "Nothing's wrong," she stated, all business and no nonsense. "Time for dinner."

Malory stared in disbelief as her mother ushered the boys out of the room. How could she do it? How could she just shut down her emotions like turning off a faucet? Tommy looked over his shoulder on the way out with his innocent, childish eyes. Malory tried to smile. She didn't want to scare the boys. They had enough to deal with without a hysterical older sister.

But her head pounded and her stomach hurt. She definitely didn't feel like eating. What she felt like doing was going back in time. Back to her afternoon with Ben, which suddenly seemed like a lifetime ago.

At this moment running away seemed like the best idea she'd had in a long, long time.

Thirteen

MALORY WAS SUPPOSED to tutor Joey the next day, but she stayed home to be with her mother. Her father had taken the day off from work, but Malory thought that her mother needed extra support. After last night's flawless performance—complete with a pleasant dinner and movie rental after—Mrs. Hunter seemed to be having a little more trouble today coping with the reality of her mother's death. But Malory was secretly relieved by her mother's depression and listlessness. It meant she was dealing with the situation—not pretending it hadn't happened.

Her father, on the other hand, continued on with his performances. She was glad that he had found a replacement for the day in order to be there for her mother, but all he did was crack jokes and tell stories about work. She knew that he was just trying to cheer her mother up, but Malory wished that he would quit his happy charades. Their life *wasn't* happy right now, and it wouldn't be for a long time. What was the point in pretending?

The sky was cloudless and blue, and there wasn't a trace of yesterday's rain on the ground—so it didn't take long for the twins to get restless. Despite the beautiful weather, Mrs. Hunter wanted Mike and Tommy to play inside. Malory couldn't tell if she was in one of her overprotective moods or if she just needed the company of those she loved. At first the boys were fine, amazingly enough. Mr. Hunter did a jigsaw puzzle with them. Then they built a house of cards. But by five-thirty they were bouncing off the walls.

"B-ball, b-ball, b-ball!" they chanted until finally Mr. Hunter agreed to play basketball with them out back.

"Let's go, guys," he said. "Honey, we'll be back in about an hour."

"Yay!" the boys whooped as they grabbed the basketball and headed for the door.

Mr. Hunter kissed Mrs. Hunter on the top of her head. "Now, Kathryn, if you need anything, I'll be right out back." Tommy and Mike were already out the door. Mr. Hunter smiled and ran out after them.

The door slammed shut. Mrs. Hunter managed a tired laugh.

"I can't believe the twins haven't been driving you nuts, Mom," Malory mumbled.

"You'll look at it differently when you have your own, Mal," she said gently.

Malory shrugged.

"They needed to get outside," Mrs. Hunter said in a faraway voice, gazing out the window. "It's too nice a day to be cooped up in here. That's one thing I love about our new home—the weather."

At the mention of the word *home,* Malory felt a nervous flutter in the pit of her stomach. She knew with sudden certainty that L.A. would not be their home for very much longer. If the FBI had contacted them about her grandmother, they would be contacting them again soon about something else. The FBI never called just once. There was always a series of calls, starting with a small reminder or piece of news, then one telling them they were "hot" or "cool"—and then a call telling them it was time to move. Maybe not in the next month—maybe not even in the next three—but soon. She tried not to think about Ben.

The telephone rang.

Malory looked at it—then back at her mother. She swallowed. Phone calls never meant anything good. Either there was an emergency . . . or someone had gotten their number.

The phone rang again, insistently, demanding to be answered.

Then Malory remembered: *Ben*. She flashed her mother what she hoped was an apologetic look, then swiftly went over to the wall phone.

"Hello," she said hopefully into the mouthpiece.

Instead of Ben's voice, there was silence. Then the phone clicked. The dial tone buzzed sharply in Malory's ear.

A chill went down her spine.

"Mal?" her mother asked.

"Wrong number," Malory muttered, not looking at her mother. She placed the phone back down on the receiver.

"Who did they ask for?" Mrs. Hunter wanted to know.

"No one—there wasn't anyone on the line."

Mrs. Hunter looked at her.

"What, what is it?" Malory snapped. "It was a wrong number. People get wrong numbers all the time. It's no big deal."

"Calm down, Malory. It just seemed like you were expecting someone to call."

Malory didn't say anything. She was disgusted with herself—both for not telling her mother the truth and for being short with her when she was so upset. What was her problem? She was just about to apologize when the phone rang again. She immediately snatched it up.

"Hello?" she breathed into the phone.

"Maddy?" Ben's voice asked.

Malory breathed a quick sigh of relief. She glanced over her shoulder at her mother, who suddenly got up and went into her bedroom. A pang of guilt shot through her, but there was nothing she could do about that now. "Hi," she whispered.

"What's up?" Ben asked in a low, intimate voice.

"Oh, not much," Malory said guardedly, afraid that her mother could hear.

"I thought about you all last night," Ben said.

Malory felt herself blushing. "Me too," she said.

"Are you okay? I was a little worried about you—"

"No, I'm fine," Malory said quickly.

There was a pause. "Do you think we can get together a little later? Maybe go to a movie or something? Or we could bike in the park. . . ."

Malory smiled sadly. It all sounded so wonderful—all of it. So far removed from the tension in this apartment. But she doubted if she could convince her mother to let her go out with Ben right now. Not to mention that Malory didn't exactly want to leave her alone at a time like this. . . .

"Or we could just go for a walk around your neighborhood, you know, get ice cream or something," Ben said in the silence. "Whatever you want to do."

Neighborhood walk. Ice cream. That sounded

sufficiently close to home. She could go out for half an hour, then come back. That wasn't so bad. Surely she could do that if the boys could play basketball downstairs.

"You know, everything you said sounds great, but . . ." Malory hesitated a moment. "I, uh, have to check with my mother."

All at once Mrs. Hunter appeared at Malory's side. "Who is it?" she mouthed.

Malory froze. She instantly decided to tell her mother the truth—and think of an excuse later. "It's Mrs. Lerner's son, Ben Lerner." She held her breath, wondering what her mother would say next.

"Maddy?" Ben asked. "Are you still there?"

"Uh, yeah," she said distractedly. "Hold on one second." She licked her lips. "Hey, Mom, is . . . it, uh, okay if I go out for like half an hour?"

She expected her mom to refuse, to fold her arms crossly, *anything*—but her mother stared at her. Finally she flashed a small, melancholy smile. "Okay," she whispered, then returned to the living room couch.

"Maddy?" Ben asked again.

"What? Yeah—I can go." Malory shook her head, still stunned by her mother's response. "Not for long, though," she added quickly.

"That's fine," he said, sounding relieved. "I'll be there in about fifteen minutes."

He hung up before Malory could even say

good-bye. She placed the phone back on the hook and looked at it for a second. She had been hoping to ask him if he'd tried to call before and gotten disconnected. It must have been either him or a wrong number. There was no other possible explanation, she comforted herself.

"Malory?" her mother called.

Malory groaned silently. She dreaded the thought of facing her mother and giving an explanation—but she forced herself to march into the living room.

"That was your music teacher's son?" Mrs. Hunter asked. She didn't look at Malory. She just sat on the couch and stared out the window.

"Yeah."

"Is he a nice boy?"

Malory was a little surprised. Usually her next question would be: *Have you told him anything I should know about?*

"Yeah . . . ," Malory said warily, not sure where the conversation was leading.

"And you like him very much?" Mrs. Hunter continued, glancing over at Malory this time.

Malory's face reddened, but she didn't say anything.

"I see," Mrs. Hunter said. "And you gave him our telephone number."

Malory nodded again. "Yeah, but Mom—"

"Well, then he must be a very special person," Mrs. Hunter interrupted softly.

Malory paused. *She knows.* Somehow, even though Malory hadn't said a single word, her mother knew that Malory had fallen in love. She couldn't go on playing a charade any longer. There was no point. It would be best to let her mother know everything. She took a deep breath. "He's the most wonderful guy I've ever met."

Mrs. Hunter's expression became troubled. "I see . . . ," she said uncertainly. "Malory—"

"Please, Mom," Malory pleaded in a whisper. "Don't start."

But her mother just shook her head. "It isn't safe. It's not safe for you, and it's not safe for him. If your father knew, he'd be furious. We could be forced to leave at a moment's notice, and you'll never be able to tell him any of it. Not ever." The words poured out of her mouth. "You wouldn't even be able to say good-bye."

Malory winced. "I know," she breathed. "I wasn't planning on this, Mom—I swear. It just happened. It wasn't anything I could control."

Her mother opened her mouth as if she were about to say something else—but then her expression softened. "I know, honey," she said after a while. "It never is."

"So where exactly *is* the ice cream parlor?" Ben asked after they had been walking for a while.

Malory glanced at him. "Uh . . . I thought *you* knew."

Their eyes locked for a moment, then Ben's face broke into a wide smile. The next thing Malory knew, they were laughing hysterically.

"Well, I like walking aimlessly," Ben said once he had regained his composure. "To be honest, I really didn't feel like ice cream anyway."

"Neither do I," Malory said. "Sorry about that, Ben. I thought you would have known. . . ."

"It's okay. I just don't know this neighborhood very well."

"Oh." Malory began walking again. For some reason, she'd assumed that Ben knew all of L.A. because he'd lived here all his life. Her eyes roved over the crumbling curbs and run-down buildings near her apartment. Now that she thought of it, Ben probably didn't have much reason to come to this part of town very often. His own neighborhood was much more pleasant.

"What's it like, growing up in the same place and living in the same house all your life?" Malory asked wistfully.

"I don't know. Boring. Ordinary," Ben said with a shrug. He looked at her curiously.

"Really? That's not how I imagine it," Malory said. "I wish I had a boring, ordinary life."

Ben's gaze intensified. Suddenly Malory realized that she had said something revealing. She swallowed.

"What do you mean?" Ben asked.

I could tell him. I could tell him about me,

and he wouldn't ever breathe a word of it, I know, Malory thought. She stopped walking. Wisps of dyed black hair stirred around her face in the breeze.

"What I mean is . . . I wish that I could have lived in the same place, right here, so I could have known you my whole life," she said quietly. "So we could have been little kids who went to the same kindergarten, then playmates, then . . ." She didn't finish. All at once she felt as if she might burst into tears.

"That would have been nice," Ben breathed. He reached over and brushed some of her hair out of her eyes. "Maddy?" Ben said tentatively.

She shivered. The air was getting colder as the sun sank lower in the sky. "Yeah?" Malory answered.

"Did you, were you . . . ?" Ben paused.

Malory took his hand. "What is it, Ben?"

"Wherever you came from, those lots of places you lived—and I'm not asking where those were," Ben said quickly. "I just mean, wherever—did you . . . ever . . ." Ben left the unfinished question hanging between them.

"Did I ever . . . what?" Malory prodded.

Ben took a deep breath.

"Did you ever tell some guy you loved him before—in wherever," Ben asked, the words tumbling out in a rush.

Malory's eyes widened.

"Never mind," he mumbled quickly, letting her hand go. He looked as if he were disgusted with himself. "It was a stupid question. You don't have to answer it."

She just stared at him. *I've never loved anyone but you,* she thought, but she just couldn't bring herself to say it. It wasn't fair—to either of them. How could she love him when she had only known him for a short while, when she knew that soon she would leave and never see him again? It wasn't logical. But even as she wrestled with these questions, she knew that logic had nothing to do with it. She *did* love him.

"No," Malory whispered. "I haven't. What . . . what about you? Have you ever told a girl you loved her?"

"Never," Ben said simply.

Malory paused. She leaned closer to him, taking his hand again and squeezing it tightly. For some reason Shella's words were flashing through her mind: *"He does this every year. He likes to pretend he's some sort of down-and-out artist. So he picks up some weird loner and pretends he's her boyfriend. It never lasts. Believe me, I've seen it before."*

"Ben, have you been involved with many girls?" she suddenly blurted.

"A few," he admitted steadily. "But never with anyone like you. You're the most . . . well, you're the most amazing girl I've ever met."

Malory just looked at him. She had no idea what to say.

"Maddy, this may sound ridiculous—but have you ever thought that maybe you don't have to go along with your parents every time they move?"

Malory's heart thumped loudly in her chest. "Wh-What do you mean?" she stammered.

"What I mean is . . . when do you say that enough is enough? When do you start living your own life?"

"I have my own life," Malory answered, for some reason feeling immediately defensive.

"Do you?" Ben demanded. "I mean, you can't live in any one place because your parents, for whatever reason, decide it's time to move. You can't even play the piano, Maddy!" His voice rose. "You have to go to some stranger's house to do the one thing you love most. Whatever it is your parents are running from, or running toward, or hiding from—or *whatever*—doesn't seem to have anything to do with you. So why do you have to keep paying for their mistakes with *your* life?"

Malory blinked, then tried to wipe the wetness from her eyes with a trembling hand. "It's my life too, Ben," she whispered.

"But you're sixteen. You should be thinking about college, and going out, and having fun, and . . . me."

I do think about you, she thought miserably. *I*

think about you more than anything else. But already she was beginning to feel that numbness she always felt when her life grew too painful to handle.

"I'm sorry," Ben said. "I don't want to put you on the spot like this. But . . . I'm worried about you, Maddy."

"I'll be fine, Ben," she murmured. "I promise."

He leaned forward and kissed her gently, and for a moment she lost herself in the sensation of his lips melting against hers. Could she really ever truly run away? Kissing Ben made her feel more wonderful than she ever could have imagined. In that instant, as his arms wrapped tightly around her body, she had a wild fantasy of breaking free from her parents and living with Ben at his house—playing his mom's piano, going to school, doing all those things she never could. . . .

But it was impossible.

She stepped away from him and took a deep breath. "I should probably be getting home," she said.

He nodded gravely. "I know."

Malory shook her head. She could never run away. She could never live with Ben. Once you were in the witness protection program, you weren't allowed to leave unless you forfeited everything—and that meant that Malory would never be able to see or speak to her mother, her father, or her brothers again. And there was no guarantee that the Mafia wouldn't come after her anyway. She knew as much as her father. Living with Ben would put him in far too much danger.

"I'll walk you to your apartment," Ben said.

They walked in silence all the way back to Malory's block, holding hands. At least she could enjoy this moment, she realized. It was more than she ever had. And that was *something*, wasn't it?

Out of the corner of her eye Malory noticed a car idling at the end of the street. It looked like the same one she had seen last night. She squinted, trying to see the license plate. But the plate was spattered and muddy. Her pulse picked up a beat. Maybe this was a different car. It was in a different spot. And there was someone sitting in the passenger seat, waiting.

"Maddy . . . ?" Ben was asking.

But then Malory saw the woman who had been wearing the sweat suit the night before walking quickly down the street. The woman got into the car. Malory breathed a sigh of relief. It was the same car—of course it was.

Forget about it. There's nothing going on. You're just spooked today, Malory told herself. She paused in front of the entrance to her building and looked at him. "What was that?"

"Oh, nothing," Ben said in an offhanded way. "I was just thinking maybe I could come upstairs and meet your folks."

Malory shook her head. But then, as if on cue,

she saw her father walking toward them. Malory frowned. *Where are the twins? Is he looking for me? What's wrong?*

"Hello, Maddy," Mr. Hunter called as he came closer. He walked over to her and kissed her on the forehead, then cast a quick glance at Ben.

"Uh, Dad, this is, uh, this is Ben Lerner," she stammered.

Mr. Hunter smiled amiably and extended his hand. "Hello."

"I'm glad to finally meet you," he said, gripping Mr. Hunter's hand firmly. "I've been wanting to introduce myself to you for a long time."

Malory's father just nodded. Then he shot Malory a look, a look that instantly said: *Something's wrong.* And then he said, "We're having guests."

Malory felt her blood run cold.

"Maddy, it's time to go in," he said. He gave Ben another quick look, then turned and marched through the door.

Malory glanced at Ben and smiled weakly. "Okay. Good night, Ben." In her sudden panic her voice sounded odd and strained. She felt as if she had just pressed a button on a recording; the words didn't belong to her.

Ben was staring at her, bewildered. "Is that it? What guests?" he asked.

"I really have to go. I'll call you later," she said, her voice breaking. Before he could say anything else, she bolted inside.

Fourteen

MALORY FUMBLED WITH the keys to the dented apartment door, her vision blurry with tears. But before she could find the right one, the door opened before her.

It wasn't her father—or anyone she had ever seen before. It was a man in a cheap, ill-fitting suit, with dark gray hair and tired brown eyes. She gave a little gasp and tried to look over his shoulder into the living room. Should she run?

"Malory?" her mom's voice called.

"Mom?"

"It's okay, Mal. We're in here."

Malory ducked away from the man in the suit and edged into the living room. There was another man in there as well—a man in a suit, who was sitting in the easy chair. It was Jeffrey Laurence. *FBI*, Malory said to herself, feeling dread overwhelm her. She knew there was only one reason why they would be here: to move them. Malory shook her head.

Nobody said a word. Her parents were on the couch. Her father's arm was around her mother, and she was twisting her wedding band around and around on her finger, rocking slightly back and forth. Mike and Tommy lay on the old braided rug on the floor, looking listless and sad.

"What's going on?" Malory asked into the thick silence.

Jeffrey Laurence rose.

"Malory." He stuck out his hand. "Remember me? I'm Jeffrey."

In a daze she took it.

"We were just talking about your new home, Malory," he said pleasantly, nodding toward the straight-backed chair.

Malory sank into it. "I see," she said blankly. "I didn't know you knew where we were, even," she added sarcastically.

"Of course we knew, Malory; we placed you here."

"Then why did you wait to tell us that my grandmother died?" she barked, unable to quell the bitter anger that surged through her.

"Malory!" her mother hissed. "Please—"

"You were too hot at that point," Jeffrey interrupted smoothly. "We got you the information as fast as we could."

161

"Yeah, I know how hot we are," Malory grumbled. "I got a pretty good idea in Lincoln Hills."

"Malory, *please*," her father said firmly. "There's no need to be rude. These people are trying to help us. These people are trying to save our lives."

Jeffrey didn't answer. There was nothing more to say. If they were trying to save the Hunters, they were doing a lousy job, Malory thought. They had mishandled the case—plain and simple. Otherwise the Hunters would have been safe a long time ago. How long had they been in L.A.? A week? How could the Mafia have found them that quickly?

Jeffrey cleared his throat. "We have been watching your family for quite some time, Malory," he said. "Since you arrived in west L.A.—"

Suddenly there was a knock on the door. The gray-haired man at the door put his hand inside his jacket—obviously reaching for his gun. Then there was another knock, then three more in quick succession. The man relaxed and opened the door.

Malory almost did a double take. It was the woman in the jogging suit. She was carrying a piece of paper. Malory gasped. It was one of Ben's sketches—the sketch he had done that first Saturday at his mother's piano.

"How did you get that?" she cried.

"It wasn't hard," the woman replied evenly. "And if we can get it, what makes you think someone else can't? You can't afford to be this careless, Malory. Too much is at stake."

"You went through my things!" she spat. "What gives you the right?"

"We have the right to do whatever it takes to keep you alive," the woman retorted.

Malory looked wildly at her parents, but their expressions were stony. "It wasn't my fault—"

"It doesn't matter," Jeffrey said quickly. "Your artist friend won't have the opportunity to draw you again. You're leaving tomorrow."

Malory froze. She was totally unprepared for this. It didn't make any sense. They couldn't be leaving so soon. . . .

"We'll stay with you until a signal is given—sometime early in the morning," Jeffrey continued. "At that point Jane and I will escort you to the handoff."

Malory looked at the lady with the sketch. She had no expression on her face.

"This is important, Malory," Jeffrey said carefully. "At this handoff you will rendezvous with safe people carrying supplies, transportation tickets, and identification."

"And hair dye," she muttered.

"That's correct, Malory—and hair dye," continued Jeffrey. "These people will provide you with everything you need to leave the country."

"Leave the country?" Malory shouted.

"Yes," continued Jeffrey. His voice was breathless now—almost desperate. "So I suggest that all of you prepare yourselves, whatever that means. You may each carry one bag."

Malory's mind was whirling—but her thoughts kept going back to the same place: *Ben.* Somehow she had to get to him. Somehow she had to tell him she was leaving. She had to let him know how she really felt.

"Will we be traveling together?" Mrs. Hunter asked quietly.

"No. You, Malory, and Michael will travel separately from Mr. Hunter and Tommy. You will meet up at an overseas location. An agent will be there with another set of new identities for you to take you to your next destination."

Mrs. Hunter nodded.

He sighed. "Well, that's about it. My information stops there."

"I . . . I can't believe this," Malory whispered. She stared at the faces of everyone in the room. They all seemed tired, but nothing really more. The woman in the jogging suit looked bored—almost annoyed. Even her mother's face had become a blank, expressionless mask. What was the matter with them? Had they all become zombies?

"What if I refuse?" Malory heard herself asking.

Mr. Hunter looked at her sharply. "Mal, what are you talking about?"

"What if I refuse?" she repeated.

Jeffrey just shook his head. "Well, Malory, I suppose that's your decision. But I have to be honest with you. Everyone who has left the program has died. Without exception. I don't estimate the odds of your surviving to be very high." His tone was dry and matter-of-fact, as if he were talking about a football game.

"Well, what do I have to live for anyway?" she shrieked. Then she leaped from her chair and bolted into her room, slamming the door behind her.

"Malory, please . . . ," her father called after her.

She buried her face in her pillow, sobbing uncontrollably. It was so unfair. For the first time in her life, she thought she might have found something worth keeping. . . .

There was a knock on the door.

"Go away!" she shouted.

The door opened anyway. Malory pulled the pillow over her head.

"Listen, Malory, I know this is hard for you." Jeffrey's disembodied voice floated above her. "But let me make one thing clear: You *are* in great danger. We know that you were approached by someone at school. That man was sent to kill you, Malory—but luckily we got to him first. After he marked you on the school grounds, he went to call his boss. We got him at the phone booth. If we hadn't been there, you and I wouldn't be having this conversation."

"Please, just get out of here," Malory wept. "Please."

"Okay. But remember—you have to pack. And I know it's early, but try to get some sleep. You'll be leaving when it's still dark."

"Get out!" Malory snapped.

She heard the door close behind her.

Without hesitating, she sat up. She wiped her face and shook her head. She was done crying. There was no way she was going to leave without seeing Ben one last time—hit men or no hit men. Quickly she stuffed her pillows and some other clothes under her covers, fashioning the lump until it vaguely resembled a person sleeping. Then she opened the window next to her bed.

The sun had sunk below the horizon; it was already getting dark. As carefully and quietly as possible she eased herself onto the windowsill and slid out onto the fire escape. Then she padded down the steps and leaped out onto the lawn in front of the building. An instant later she recovered her balance and dashed to the telephone booth at the end of the street.

Please be there, Malory begged desperately as she shoved a quarter into the slot and dialed Ben's number. After two rings there was a click.

"Hello?" Ben asked.

Relief flooded through her. "Ben, it's me," she whispered. "I have to see you. Can you meet me?"

"Where are you?" Ben's voice was immediately urgent, worried.

"I'm on the corner at the end of my street."

"I'll come pick you up. Wait right there—"

"Ben, no! Not here!" Malory hissed.

"Maddy, what's wrong? Are you okay?" Ben's voice quavered with worry.

"I'm fine, but I can't meet you here. Meet me at—"

"I'll meet you behind the Unocal 76," Ben said.

"Fine. I'll see you there."

This was a bad idea, Malory thought, shifting on her feet in the harsh, fluorescent glare of the lights behind the gas station. She felt as if she were on a stage, in a spotlight. Every time a car drove by her, she would lurch forward excitedly. But twenty minutes had already passed, and Ben was nowhere to be seen. Night had fallen completely.

Malory hoped her parents hadn't decided to sneak into her room. She knew it wouldn't be long before they found out she was missing. And when that happened . . . well, she didn't even want to think about that.

A pair of headlights began to creep slowly up

the street. Malory squinted at them. They were too low and too far apart to belong to Ben's Jeep. Sweat trickled down her forehead. The lights slowed and slowed, creeping past her at a bare crawl. The car was a dark sedan with tinted windows. She looked at the plates. New York.

I'm dead, she said to herself.

Suddenly another pair of headlights caught her eye—a pair she instantly recognized.

"Ben!" she cried out loud. As fast as she could she sprinted down to the end of the street, half expecting bullets to fly by her. Ben threw open the passenger door as she skidded to a halt.

"Maddy, what's—"

"Drive! Drive!" she yelled as she dove in, slamming the door behind her. She ducked down in her seat.

"Maddy, what's going on?" he asked as the Jeep continued down the block.

"See that car right there?" Malory hissed.

Ben nodded nervously.

"Lose it," she commanded.

For the next few minutes Ben drove in silence while Malory crouched low between the seat and the dashboard. She was shaking violently. How did they know she was here—by the gas station? Had they seen her escape her house?

"Okay, Maddy, I don't see the car anymore," Ben said finally. He glanced at the rearview mirror, and the Jeep began to pick up speed. "You can get up now."

"You sure?" Malory asked.

He nodded.

With a grunt Malory pushed herself back up into the seat and took a deep breath. They were on a highway now—the same highway that led to the canyon. The sedan was nowhere in sight.

"Thanks, Ben," she said after a minute.

"Maddy—are you in trouble with the police?" Ben suddenly asked.

She shook her head. "It's much, much worse than that."

He didn't say anything.

"Look—I'll tell you everything," she whispered. "Just as soon as we get somewhere out of the way, somewhere quiet—"

"The canyon?" he suggested.

"Perfect."

Fifteen

MALORY AND BEN sat on the ledge overlooking the ocean. They had scrambled up in the darkness, but now they sat before a great expanse of dark blue night sky and moonlight. A few lights twinkled on the mountain, and Malory thought of all the people in their homes who felt safe and happy.

Ben sat cross-legged in front of her, looking her in the eyes, holding her hand. She knew she had to tell him now.

"I didn't want to tell you this story," she began, "and I've put it off for a long time. Not because I think you won't like me or anything, but because when I tell you the story, I'll be putting you in danger. But I think . . . that I have to tell you now."

Ben just nodded. His eyes were unflinching.

"I don't care, Maddy. I have to know the truth."

She took a deep breath. "My name's not Maddy Mailer."

He blinked.

"It's Malory Hunter."

"What are you—"

"I had to change it. My family's in the federal witness protection program."

Ben let out a deep breath. "Oh, man . . ."

"A long time ago—eleven years ago—my father was an accountant," Malory explained softly. "He worked for a big accounting firm. Like, the biggest in New York. Anyway, one of his clients was the head of the Carlotti family. Have you ever heard of them?"

Ben's jaw dropped. "You mean . . . the Mob?"

"That's right."

"And . . . your father worked for them?"

"Sort of," Malory admitted. "But he didn't even know it. He's an accountant—just a bean counter, he calls it—and he had no idea that he was doing it for the Mafia. But then he noticed that the numbers weren't adding up. So he started asking around. He and this other guy."

Ben shook his head, a terrified, confused expression on his face.

"Then his boss told them not to worry about it. My father agreed—because he wanted to keep his job. He knew something was wrong, but he wanted to protect us. But the other guy wouldn't listen. He kept asking questions." Malory's voice fell to a low whisper. "He kept asking and asking—until they shot him dead right in front of his house."

Ben squeezed Malory's hand tightly. "What happened to your father?" he breathed.

"Well, he couldn't take it anymore, and he went to the police. The police turned him over to the FBI."

"And now they're protecting you?" Ben asked.

Malory laughed bitterly. "That's the theory. But it doesn't quite work that way."

"What do you mean?"

"Somehow the Carlottis always manage to find us. From the very first moment. I mean, we almost got burned alive in New York. I was five years old, and Mike and Tommy were little babies. When the Carlottis found out my father had turned state's evidence, they didn't waste any time coming after us—even before the FBI had worked out the final details of our relocation." Malory shook her head in disgust. "They burned the whole building with one big firebomb. They did it from the basement up, hoping to burn us all up too."

Ben pulled Malory close against him, hugging her as tightly as she had ever been held before. "I am so sorry," he murmured. "I am so sorry. . . ."

Malory closed her eyes, trying to enjoy the

feeling of Ben's arms around her—even if it was only fleeting. "For the last eleven years we've been moving all over the country. It doesn't matter where we go, Ben. We went to Wyoming, Nebraska, Minnesota—it doesn't make one damn bit of difference. They always find us." A tear slid down Malory's cheek and onto Ben's shirt.

"It's okay," Ben said softly. "It's okay."

"It's *not* okay," Malory said angrily as Ben stroked her hair. "The federal witness protection program is, like, a contradiction in terms. Especially when it comes to mobsters with a lot of money."

Ben sighed. "You're so brave, Mad—I mean, Malory." He sighed softly. "You know, I never really quite believed your name was Maddy anyway. You always sounded funny when you said it."

Malory forced herself to pull away from him. "Ben—that isn't all."

He looked pale. "It isn't?"

She shook her head. "I'm leaving tomorrow morning."

"What?" he cried.

Malory looked away. She couldn't stand to see his face.

"Where are you going?" he asked after a moment.

"I don't know. All I know is that we're leaving the country."

Ben turned away and looked out at the ocean.

He put his face in his hands, then ran them through his brown hair. "I don't believe this," he said, seemingly to himself. "I'm never going to see you again. You appeared out of nowhere, then—*poof*—you're gone. It's like . . . you were a dream I had."

She reached out for him, caressing his cheek gently. "No, Ben. I wasn't a dream. I was real. And the way I feel about you is real too."

He grabbed her hand and kissed it tenderly. Tears were streaming down her cheeks now. "I love you, Ben," she choked out.

"Wait, Malory—you know, you don't have to go with them," he said desperately. "You could stay here, you could stay with my family. You could finish high school. You could go to college—you could go to Juilliard and study music. You could have a normal life. Your parents might even want that for you. . . ." His voice trailed off.

But Malory was shaking her head. Even if her family wanted that for her, she knew she could never abandon them. And staying at the Lerners' was just an impossible dream—a last, hopeless effort on Ben's part to somehow prevent the inevitable. "No," she said. "I can't leave my family. I just can't."

"Will I be able to reach you?" he asked.

Malory shook her head again. "No. I may able to call you . . . but not for a long time."

Ben's jaw was quivering. His eyes were wet. "So this is it," he whispered.

"No," Malory said adamantly. "It's not. Because someday, I don't know when—this is all going to end. I'm going to have a normal life. And I'm going to come back here and play your mom's piano while you sit on the floor and sketch those beautiful landscapes, and . . ."

Ben threw his arms around her again. She ran her fingers through his hair feverishly, kissing his neck. And at that moment she truly believed that she wasn't just having a wild daydream. At that moment she truly believed she would return to L.A. and pick up where she had left off with Ben—but *this* time without any lies, without any fear.

"I love you, Malory," Ben said.

Malory smiled. *Ben Lerner loves me,* she said to herself, repeating it over and over. And for that one, shining moment she felt like the luckiest person on earth.

It was nearly one A.M. by the time Ben's Jeep rolled to a stop in front of the Hunters' apartment.

"Are there any cars around?" Malory whispered from her crouched position under the dashboard.

"Two," he said. "An old Dodge Dart and another one . . ."

"Does the other one have California plates?" Malory asked.

"I can't see," Ben said, squinting. "It's too dark. The plates are covered with mud or something. . . ."

"That's the one," Malory said. She slithered up into her seat and glanced out the window at her apartment. The lights were still on. She could see the silhouetted shapes of people pacing around inside behind the curtains.

They're probably worried sick, she said to herself.

Ben looked at her. "What time is your flight?" he asked.

She shook her head. "I don't know. I probably won't find out until the last possible second."

He nodded. Before he could say anything else, Malory leaned over and kissed him.

"Never forget me, Ben," she whispered.

His eyes were glistening in the pale, dim light of the streetlamps. "How could I ever forget someone like you, Malory?"

She swallowed. "Ben—if for any reason, anyone comes around . . . you know, and asks about me or something. . . ." Malory stumbled over her words, fearful of what she was going to say. "Just tell them—"

"That I never heard of Malory Hunter," Ben finished for her. "I promise. You don't have to worry about me."

She smiled sadly. "I know I don't. You're going to be a famous artist and travel the world and have all the things you want in life."

A single tear slid down Ben's cheek. "All but one," he said.

She kissed him once more, then dashed out of the Jeep and closed the door behind her—and with it, she shut Ben Lerner out of her life forever.

Epilogue

"FINAL BOARDING CALL for British Airways flight number 484, nonstop to London, gate eighteen," a crisp, female British voice echoed throughout the airport. "This is the final call for all passengers on flight number 484."

At that moment a woman and her young son were part of a small group of people being hustled onto flight 484 by several men in dark suits. Two of the men boarded with them. There was no way someone in the airport might have suspected that the group was waiting for that particular flight because they had been at another gate halfway across the terminal until just two minutes ago.

They were the last passengers on flight 484 before the gate was closed.

This group would change flights again in

London and again at their next destination, wherever that might be, en route to Vienna.

Mrs. Hunter and Tommy were seated in a row in business class.

Across the aisle, alone in a window seat, sat Malory. She knew she would love the city. She knew she would never tire of walking the streets Mozart had walked and seeing what he saw . . . the old architecture, the history . . . it was going to be a new start in the perfect place.

They would be safe at last. And that was all that mattered.

And maybe, just maybe Ben really would follow through with his wish of going to Vienna to paint. He had just mentioned it casually, but maybe he really would go, and they would see each other again.

She could hope, couldn't she?

Do you ever wonder about falling in love? About members of the opposite sex? Do you need a little friendly advice but have no one to turn to? Well, that's where we come in . . . Jenny and Jake. Send us those questions you're dying to ask, and we'll give you the straight scoop on life and love in the nineties.

DEAR JAKE

Q: *My best friend, Liz, and I always end up liking the same guys. Right now our victim is this guy named Dave. Dave acts as if he likes both of us, so I can't tell how he really feels.*

He told a bunch of our friends that Liz is his girlfriend. When I asked Liz about it, she said she didn't know what I was talking about. Then Dave told me he just hangs around with her because she's cool. When Liz isn't around, he acts like we're going out. He's never been out on a real date with either one of us.

I don't know what to do. Half of me feels like I'm betraying my friend and the other half doesn't. Please help!

AA, Baltimore, MD

A: The reason you feel like you're being torn in half is because you are. This kid is not only confusing you and Liz—but he's causing a major split between best friends.

Keep in mind that he might not be causing this

confusion on purpose. He sounds as if he's pretty confused about what he wants himself. When a guy is in a situation like this, he feels really trapped. He's probably thinking that if he chooses one of you, he risks losing the other. If he's forced to make a choice and it doesn't work out, he's got no one.

What you should do is talk to Liz. You two have to figure out if either of you wants to be Dave's safety net. I can't predict whether one or both of you will give him up, but at least the situation will be out in the open. Hopefully you and Liz won't let *his* confusion break up *your* friendship.

Q: *I used to go out with this guy named Nick. We saw each other for a while, but I broke up with him about a month ago. My family had been going through a lot of trouble and I guess I just felt like I couldn't handle anything—least of all a boyfriend.*

Now that things are back to normal at home, I realize how much I miss Nick. I can't even really remember how I lost him or what made me end it. His friends say he was really upset when we broke up. I hope this means that we still have a chance. But what if I hurt him too much? How should I approach him?

QQ, Houston, TX

A: The best way to handle this situation is to take a deep breath and call him. Tell him you just want to talk. Start out with an apology. Tell him you're sorry you ended things so quickly and ask for a chance to explain the reasons.

Try to be honest about your family problems. You don't have to tell him every little detail if you don't want to. Tell him enough to explain how confused, upset, and preoccupied you were. It sounds as if you really like each other, so hopefully he'll be mature enough to understand that you had a lot on your mind.

Once you explain, your relationship will be even stronger than before.

Q: *Why is it that whenever I feel like I'm getting close to a boy, he acts like he doesn't like me anymore?*

I have a crush on this guy named Jeff. We flirted with each other for a long time. Then, just as we stopped being silly and really started to get to know each other, he backed off. And the thing is, this happens to me all the time!

I don't think I'm being pushy or overbearing. In fact, I'm really patient. What am I doing to scare these guys off?

CS, Sacramento, CA

A: I can't even begin to tell you how many of these letters we get a month. So—for all of you ladies out there with this same question, let me just tell you one thing: You are not scaring them off!

Young men are very fickle. They start to like a girl, and when they're in that flirting stage, they're right there with you, enjoying themselves. But then one little thing can strike fear in their hearts. It could be something you do at the time—a smile, a touch of the hand, a toss of your hair over your shoulder, and *boom!*—they're seeing public hand holding, exchanging jewelry, secret note passing during biology class . . . and, well, they panic.

The point is that guys scare themselves off. One guy may really like you—but he may be scared that his friends will pick on him, or that you might want to take up all his time, or that he'll be seen as a wuss. Sooner or later they will mature to the point where *they* will want relationships as much as you do. For some guys that age is thirteen and for others it's upward of eighty-five. Be patient!

DEAR JENNY

Q: *This guy, we'll call him Seth, asked me out earlier in the year. He's three years older than me, so I wasn't sure at first. Finally I said yes. We went out for about three months, and then I found out he was cheating on me. Before I even had a chance to get mad at him, he broke up with me.*

A few months later he broke up with the girl he dumped me for. People started saying he liked me again. We fooled around a little bit, but then he asked someone else to the prom. The weird thing is, I still really like him. He's such a player—but he's so good looking and he really is a nice guy. I'm so confused!

AL, Xenia, OH

A: I have to be direct on this one. Get this guy out of your system as fast as possible. You were right when you said he's a player. Think about that word for a minute. If he's a player, that makes you the toy. He's using you for fun. That makes him far from being a "nice guy."

Seth obviously cares about no one but himself. If he did, he wouldn't have cheated on you in the first place. He wouldn't have fooled around with you, knowing he was going to ask someone else to the prom. Good-looking or not, this one is not worthy of a place in your heart.

Q: *My neighbor Jared and I have been friends since we were four years old. We played together all the time back then, but when I was six years old, I found out I had cancer. After that we didn't see each other much.*

Now I'm thirteen and have been in remission for four years. He just turned fifteen, and I have a big crush on him. I know he likes me, but he is very, very shy. He would never show it unless I take the first step. I've written him a long letter, but he is too shy to respond.

I'm also worried about two things. I'm nervous and scared about our height difference. I'm about five inches shorter than him because of what happened to my spinal cord when I had radiation treatment. I'm also worried because he'll be in high school in the fall while I'm stuck in eighth grade. Should I be worried about this stuff?

SM, Portland, OR

A: You are a very brave girl. You survived a horrible disease and subsequent treatment at a very young age. I'm sure that's given you the confidence and courage you show in going after the older guy you want.

On that note, you should also be confident in your appearance and your ability to maintain a relationship even if you are in different schools. It is not out of the ordinary for couples to have big height differences. My aunt is five inches taller than my uncle! If Jared likes you as much as you say he does, he won't care about the height difference or meeting you halfway between his school and yours.

To help him get over his shyness, you might want to ask him to go out with a group of friends—guys and girls—so he has more people to talk to and less to be tense about. You can also be sneaky and try "accidentally" bumping into him. Tell him you're on your way to get an ice-cream cone and ask him to join you. He might enjoy the spontaneity.

Q: *For the past few months my friends and I have been teased by a group of older guys at school. One of them, Shu Chuan, likes to tease me more than the others. Naturally I got angry and told all my girlfriends he was a jerk.*

Now, I guess because I talk about him so much, all my friends think I like him, and they're teasing me about it. I told them it's not true . . . but the problem is, it really is true. I don't understand it! Somewhere along the line I must have started liking him. What's really strange is, we both have bad tempers, so we end up quarreling almost all the time. Still, I can't stop thinking about him. What should I do?

JN, Singapore

A: You've just demonstrated the thin line between love and hate. Sometimes teasing can turn into flirtation without the players even realizing it. This is what happened to you and Shu Chuan— and it isn't all that strange. You probably enjoy the attention and the challenge that this older, hot-tempered guy presents.

You might feel strange about admitting your new crush to your friends, but since they already suspect it, they'll probably get over the shock pretty fast. The real problem is deciding whether to pursue a relationship with someone who always keeps you arguing.

Consider what your conversations are really like. Is this constant quarreling really good-natured, flirtatious bickering? Or do you two have knock-down-drag-out fights? If you'll always be at odds, you probably shouldn't pursue the relationship. You don't want to always be angry with your significant other. But if it's just silliness, go for it.

Feel confident knowing he's already singled you out. That's a good sign.

Do you have questions about love? Write to:

Jenny Burgess or Jake Korman
c/o Daniel Weiss Associates
33 West 17th Street
New York, NY 10011